Praise for
The Musici

"What an incredibly inspiring journey it has been with dearest Heloisa Prieto, one of Brazil's most celebrated authors! Her book *The Musician* is inspired by troubadours and found its way into words through a narrative imprinted by a deep poetical exchange that we have immersed ourselves in since 2019. This captivating fiction narrates a story of a young musician whose life encounters dramatic and powerful turns after his magical musical secret has been revealed. Deep gratitude to Heloisa and to the Source of Life allowing us to experience all forms of creativity and heartfelt encounters!"

—Estas Tonne

"Heloisa Prieto is a story finder and storyteller who creates an alternative place in our world. *The Musician* expands our everyday perceptions so that we can enter a reality that is in tune with the symphony of life that is whole, real, and surrounds our everyday mundane reality.

It's also an introduction of how to quiet the everyday chatter, to question what is real, and what is important in our cultures and on our planet."

—Elaine Reardon, author of *The Heart Is a Nursery for Hope* and
Look Behind You

"*The Musician* is a beautifully crafted story involving elements of the supernatural, reminiscent of Edgar Allan Poe. Heloisa Prieto's pen draws with bold strokes a kaleidoscope of characters in this unique story, explosive in its power to wrap the reader in a fabric of tension which is compelling and alive."

—Claire Galligan, international award-winning theater director, radio producer, and writer

"*The Musician* is a charmingly unique story that feels, at times, as if Prieto had asked the question 'What would happen if I wrote a classic Latin American magical realism story but gave it a quirky ensemble cast a lá Wes Anderson?' The result is a heartwarming portrait of modern-day Brazil as seen from the eyes of diverse characters both young and old, city folk, and Indigenous forest folk alike. The thread that connects them all and winds itself arounds readers' hearts is the magical music at the core of the tale."

—Danielle Koehler, author of *The Other Forest*

"There is magic in music, and Heloisa Prieto's elegant prose captures the marriage of the two in a fanciful narrative that also touches the heart's most profound truths. Accessible, readable, subtle, and often delightful, *The Musician* draws us forward with a fresh tale that carries deep messages of time, place, and the integrity inherent in each soul, to be read slowly and savored for its whimsy and its wisdom."

—Greg Fields, author of *Through the Waters and the Wild*, 2022 Winner, Independent Press Award for Literary Fiction

"*The Musician* presents ordinary people connected in an unordinary way. But make no mistake. These people might look ordinary, but the reason they got together has to do with their peculiar qualities and search for self-discovery. Add some singing creatures, forest dwellers, magical secrets, and medieval musical sheets; whispers of ancient magic, premonitions, and astral travels that explore parallel worlds. Are you hooked? So, I still must mention the narrative that places all extraordinary creatures and their mysteries as if they were pieces of a puzzle.

"As we connect to the narrative, we become keepers of an enchanted thread that will encompass ideas, words, characters, mysteries, and infinite possibilities, until our reading heart will, finally, be caught. Softly. As the most beautiful melodies that seduce one's soul."

—Flavia Muniz, author of *The Travelers of Infinite*

"When I read *The Musician*, several emotions overwhelmed me and sometimes even transfixed me. Books by Heloisa Prieto seem to have this effect on me, as if they could fragment my perceptions, turning them into kaleidoscopes allowing me to read them through more angles, more characters, so that I could have more lives to live in a hundred pages. . . . But, as we all know, a book always goes beyond its own pages. Every book is also made of what we, the readers, make of it and can only be completed once it is read, a move that only belongs to its reader. So, I could, but choose not to, speak too much of Heloisa Prieto's brilliant writing technique. I still need to address the emotions *The Musician* made me feel when I realized the book held a magical gate to bridge Brazilian Indigenous cultures to readers abroad."

—Dr. Katia Charada, PhD in literary theory and history at the University of Campinas

"Some are born with eyes to see, while others are not.

"A scriptwriter who seizes stories around her, a lonely musician whose inspiration comes from musical creatures, kids who have premonitions, and Indigenous people who can listen to Nature's music are some of the characters who can see beyond everyday life. As a counterpoint, talent-sucking vampires, people who cannot see beyond frivolities, and a skeptical lady who has always been critical of her mother's mystical beliefs.

"In *The Musician*, as well as in *Lenora* and *Ian*, Heloisa Prieto's previous novels, the plot brings to the table issues such as the beauty and burden of being a genuine creative genius, someone whose sensitivity can actively open unknown realms, as well as its risks. At the end of the day, no one remains immune to one's true talent's impact."

—Gabriella Mancini, selected for the Bolsa da Fundación Carolina in Madrid (2008), the Havana Festival in Cuba (2007), as well as the Sesame Street Lab TV Cultura (2014)

"I really appreciated reading Heloisa Prieto's *The Musician*. I believe it is very relevant for people to get acquainted with our cultural scenario and traditional wisdom. According to Guarani teachings, artists don't do their job just to entertain, but to touch people's hearts. We say that writers are warriors, in the sense that they are God gifted, so I believe her book will be very important as a way to show contemporary society a different world: ours."

—Olivio Jekupé, Indigenous writer from the Guarani nation has published twenty-four books, including bilingual editions (Guarani Portuguese), such as *Tekoa, Meeting an Indigenous Village, The Real Saci,* and *Jaxy Jatere's Gift.*

"Heloisa Prieto's poetic, magical tale—a love story—reveals the portrait of the artist as a musician. Its storyline, with moments of great tension, is enriched by many layers of significance due to allusions to authors, poems, songs, and myth, as that of Orpheus. The narrative's main theme, 'the world is full of magic things, patiently waiting for our senses to grow sharper,' mentioned by one of the characters, alludes to Yeats's deep interest in symbolism and myth.

"Blending different settings such as the center of a metropolis and the forest and its voices, the story reaches many levels of perception of reality and fantasy."

—Dr. Munira Hamud Mutran, Doctor Honoris Causa on Literature,
National University of Ireland, Maynooth

"Let your mind be mesmerized by the magic this book can unravel. Walk on through Heloisa Prieto's delicate text upon a world in which magic and reality are so blended that they become an indivisible unity.

"As an author of books that have become essential to Brazilian literature, here Heloisa creates unforgettable characters . . . a narrative which by the magic of music leads us to re-signify the classic Greek myth of Orpheus intertwined [with] the fight for the Indigenous forest people preservation and the urgent need to face the ecological issue that is threatening our planet. The characters of this entrancing book shall transform you, in one way or the other."

—Maria José Silveira, acclaimed Brazilian author of *Her Mother's Mother & Her Daughters*, awarded the Outstanding First Novel prize by São Paulo's Critics Association

The Musician

by Heloisa Prieto

ISBN 978-1-64663-862-8

Published by

 köehlerbooks™

3705 Shore Drive
Virginia Beach, VA 23455
800-435-4811
www.koehlerbooks.com

THE
MUSICIAN

HELOISA PRIETO

VIRGINIA BEACH
CAPE CHARLES

To my dear friends Karai Papa Mirim, Olivio Jekupe, Maria Kerexu, Aparício, Kamila Pará Mirim, Owera, Tupã Mirim, Ailton Krenak, Kaká Werá, and Daniel Munduruku, and to my family, Lia, Leonardo, Guilherme, Augusto, Claudia Guedes, Tuca, and Priscila Nemeth.

Preface

In a world full of contradictions, the subtle movement of a storyline is ongoing. This is the story of a human living throughout the ages, evolving into something hard to imagine. What truly develops, perhaps, is consciousness itself. Certain aspects of human nature didn't change over the ages. Greed, jealousy, control, and manipulation are as present as ever—but so are qualities like sharing, support, adventure, love, and kindness. The difference between the Middle Ages and Ancient Greece compared to today's reality is enormous, especially in the amount of information and its ease of accessibility. Certain qualities we as humans have lost, and some we have found.

Observing the process of writing this wonderful book by my dear friend, Heloisa Prieto, I could cinematically experience the development of the chapters and characters. May it be a musician, a teacher, little brothers, a lost soul, or a native girl and her grandfather—they all came to live here and vividly expressed their uniqueness. What does life teach us daily? What purpose do stories play in our day-to-day life? Each perspective provides a way to learn about this world, life in general, and ourselves most of all.

I have a feeling that readers will be taken on a journey where the archetypes that represent "good" and "bad" qualities are vividly reflected on these pages. Such a mirror is an excellent opportunity for humankind to see that everyone participates in a grand story called *life*, where all opposites have a role to play and where *knowing* is *remembering.*

Such observation might eventually lead us to ask ourselves a fundamental question. What is the magical sound of a soul's calling that brought YOU here, singing your unique song of eternity?

—Estas Tonne

THOMAS'S JOURNAL

FOUR SECRETS

The world is inhabited by all kinds of creatures.

Some creatures are strange; some are not.

Some strange creatures are real; some are not.

In order to really see the world as it is, forget words like "strange," "real," or "imaginary."

SECRET SOUNDS

Thomas was on the verge of a panic attack. Everything seemed to be madly out of control. Why? He inhaled slowly, his mind trying to capture the exact moment when things went wrong.

Before leaving home, he had carefully placed all his papers in separate suitcases. He'd known something seemed out of order when, moments after he worked, the beautiful dream he experienced had been erased from his mind. It definitely wasn't a good sign. He surveyed his hall. A space crowded with sofas and tables made him uncomfortable. He rarely had guests, but when they did appear, they would call him a minimalist. Secretly, they thought his habits were unusual but were careful never to say this to his face. Books and notebooks were piled carefully and spread around the space looking like small, colorful buildings. Low, wooden tables were also covered by books, except for one, the one Thomas used for his meals. There were hardly any chairs; he enjoyed reading, playing, and eating cross-legged on the shiny floor with its scattering of Asian rugs. Numerous musical instruments were leaned against the white walls like trees in a musical forest.

Thomas kept his collection of suitcases near the entrance door, always ready for travel. The largest suitcase, a chestnut brown color, held his journals, the black suitcase his documents, and a red one for all his appointment books, old and new. A green suitcase held lists of things yet to come, and the gray suitcase was for pictures, fragments of ideas, and puzzling, visionary dreams. The smallest suitcase, more so a handbag, held sketches, photos from his childhood, beautiful skies, mountains, lakes, moons, stars, and the sea.

He touched them all, feeling relief flood his body. Everything seemed to be under control. He glanced at his cell phone. There was plenty of time to have a cup of coffee. Thomas looked at his luggage once more before going to the kitchen. The suitcases were all still. No creatures tried to flee from his pages. He took a deep breath. For as long as he could remember, he had the ability to see and hear musical beings. As a baby, still in his crib, he sensed their presence as sound and shadows. Moving musical shadows, so friendly and beautiful, he spent hours watching them dance around him. It was years before he realized other children, more particularly, adults, couldn't see or hear his sweet melodic friends.

"My son loves his invisible friends," his mother would tell the teachers, who assumed he was a crazy little boy. "A lot of kids have invisible pals. It is quite normal," his mother would insist.

It was useless. Thomas had never felt like the teachers treated him the same as the other children.

Forcing his memories aside, Thomas looked out of the window. It was such a lovely day. He put on his black coat and his black hat, covering his long dark hair. He looked in the mirror and smiled. They were always with him, the musical creatures. Secret creatures of sound. In the short glance in the mirror, he saw several beings smiling back at him. They danced in and out of the mirror so fast that he could barely follow their cute little movements.

There was something different about today, though—he could sense it. A lifetime spent in the company of music had enlarged his mind and heart. However, he had not fully developed his own musical eyes. He could sense so many things, even the future, but not predict it. He knew eyes were supposed to see, not to hear. But what would happen when they could?

Thomas took a while to decide which guitar he would play that Sunday. Each instrument held its own secret. Besides, he wasn't sure whether he would play music, write, or draw in his notebooks. All he really wanted to do was sit on a bench by the fountain and let the sun's rays caress his face while he watched his musical creatures bathe in the sparkling waters. He wanted to enjoy being alive—enjoy being himself.

The cab pulled up outside. Thomas glanced back at the hall, realizing he'd left his Spanish guitar against the wall. It would be his companion for the day. He picked up the black suitcase, placed his guitar on his back, and climbed into the waiting taxi.

It was lunchtime. Thomas loved watching people sitting down for family meals, chatting, taking a break from work, and sharing the daily news. He wondered how it would feel to have a normal, predictable life, knowing that he would never find out. In some ways, he longed to be like everyone else, living just twenty-four hours a day. But his curiosity for exploring, finding new places and lands, always kept him on the road. He knew he loved walking the path of traveling musicians. Every time he crossed borders, he felt a longing to enter a timeless land. A peaceful place with no borders, no beginnings, no endings. Life as it really was.

WRITTEN CONSTELLATIONS

Marlui longed to feel the rain with her fingers. She traced the lines created by the droplets on the window, realizing that she'd never feel the raindrops from inside the train.

"Rain child"—this is what her grandfather Popygua called her. In her village, in the heart of the rainforest, everyone had two names—the official one, for documents, and the secret, magical one.

Her name had been revealed by her ancestors during a long ceremony. Marlui and two other girls were blessed with musical prayers. Popygua, her grandfather and healer, stood before them and chanted while the three of them sat by the riverbank.

The sun was setting, and Marlui remembered being mesmerized by its intense, shifting rays. She'd never forget it— there she was, enjoying the sound of Popygua's strong voice when, suddenly, she could picture it: the third riverbank, the realm of her ancestors. She couldn't actually see the huge trees or swaying green branches, nor could she hear the stunning songs of birds. She couldn't even grasp the words spoken by her late great-grandmother, who was there, alive again, just smiling and waving at her. It was not a vision breaking through reality and imposing itself on her mind. It wasn't a regular dream either; her eyes were wide open. Marlui had felt as if a new realm had been revealed to her, a secret land the river would not unveil easily, and a gift for her eyes only.

Soft drops of rain had fallen over her hair as Popygua caressed her head. "Smiling Raindrop. That's your secret name," he said. "But I will call you my rainchild. It will be your nickname. I will teach you how to connect to the Rain Spirits, my girl."

From that moment on, the third river would always spray its magical drops into her eyes, and it was as if she were able to inhabit two parallel worlds. Most of the time, she felt empowered and privileged for having two realities at her disposal, but there were days when she had to be careful not to forget the other world, not to miss her step on the stairs at the train station, not to share her secrets with people who could only see and relate to one single reality.

She gazed through the train window and ran her fingers along the raindrops, drawing shapes. A long fishtail stretched into an owl head with large monkey arms—the strangest combination rain had ever given her. It disappeared suddenly as a page covered the window, wet and clinging. Words melted against the glass. Star poems. Words toppling out from their written constellations. Another page followed, stuck, and vanished just as quickly. Marlui wished the words and images would stay on the glass long enough for her to grasp their meanings. But it was not to be.

Marlui left the train station and headed downtown. Still puzzled by the dissolving poems, she tried to push the thoughts away. She had so much to do today, chores that needed to be done, such as collecting her documents for her classes at the university, buying some toys for the kids in the village, and getting her grandfather a warm blanket. But first, she wanted to buy herself an ice cream and sit quietly by the fountain square. She didn't like the traffic. She always thought there were far too many people on the streets, and she missed the quietness of her forest whenever she went to the city. Except for the fountain square, she loved the birds, the older folk playing dame or chess, the painters selling portraits, children dancing around, and the music. There was always music on the square.

On that particular day, Marlui arrived at the fountain just as a young man had taken his guitar out. He was sitting on the bench, with his back to the fountain, two boys beside him. Marlui looked for a place on another bench beside them. He took off his black hat to greet her, and she smiled back. He tuned his guitar, and when he started playing, she felt as if his music was greeting her also.

Without warning, a gust of wind swooped in and stole his notebook away. Post-its and loose pages took to the air. The two boys leaped off the bench and sprinted in all directions, trying to catch the small pieces of paper. She watched as people who caught the pages stared down at the words, mesmerized. Nobody was throwing them away, she realized, and no one seemed to be returning them to the young musician either. It was as if the pages held them in some sort of secret spell.

Marlui wanted to hug him. She understood his loss, but she didn't understand the theft. Why hadn't people returned his treasured pages? Why keep them?

Marlui closed her eyes and prayed for the rain to silence the wind. It was not an easy prayer. Not as easy as calling the rain down. Rain spirits loved dancing on earth, but to push them back into the sky, she would have to promise them her dreams. It would mean at least three sleepless nights. Marlui hesitated, but then a page landed beside her on the bench. A drawing. The head of a black dragon holding a treasure in his mouth—an exceptionally beautiful instrument, half guitar, half flute.

Marlui whispered to the rain spirits. The wind went away. In her mind's eye, she could see the rain spirits dancing upward, crossing the horizon, and leaving rainbows behind. She smiled.

The young musician sat back on the bench, placing his journal and its loose pages securely at his side. He started playing again. The tune changed; a sweet lullaby floated through the air. He stared at her and smiled as if to say thank you. As if he could sense the rain spirits taking away the clouds. How could he? Marlui smiled back at him and let his music take her on a lovely journey somewhere above the clouds.

THOMAS'S JOURNAL

Guarani

Krenak

Bororo

Munduruku

Pataxo

Potiguara

Tukano

Surui Pater

Terena

Xavante

Yanomani

Krahô

There are at least 305 indigenous nations in Brazil.

ANDRÉ AND MANUEL

Some people just know dragons are for real. They are born knowing.

For little André, dragons did not only belong in fairy-tale caves. Dragons could also fly near skyscrapers. André saw dragons in the city sky, his eyes finding them on windowpanes and windshields, traveling on the winter winds and into his heart.

Dragons, he knew, were shape shifters. They could become composite dragons, half children, half regular animals, like dogs and cats, half magical, and half real. He'd known from a young age that people never seemed to see the same things. Some are born with eyes to see, while others are not. For André, the fact that his brother Miguel could see them too made him happy.

It was during his eighth birthday party that he realized Miguel shared the gift of sight. Miguel had been breaking all the toys, removing their heads, arms, wheels, and wings. His mother begged him to stop, growing more frustrated until she watched him begin to make new toys out of the mess he'd created. He mixed the parts in the most unexpected ways. Plastic horses had fish tails, and human bodies had dragon heads and dog paws. He produced a whole collection of weird combinations that somehow worked so well.

André and Miguel's toys also transformed themselves into other beings, always to the sound of music. Their room filled with melodies only they could hear. Even when their mother complained that Miguel would rather spend all night inventing new toys than sleeping peacefully, the brothers kept their secret. They knew adults would never believe in the shifting toys musical game.

Gabriella was so proud of her two boys, and every night when she went into their room to tuck them in, she'd think, *My two angels are so lovable and adored by everyone. They are such irresistible children.*

One day after school, the boys insisted on going to the fountain square. Gabriella wondered why and asked, "André, are you studying city monuments at school?"

"No."

"What do you want to do at the fountain square?"

"I want to make a new friend. I will meet him and give him a toy."

"At the fountain? How come? Who is he?"

"I don't really know his name," André said. "I just know which toy to give him."

"This is so crazy. Even for a dreamy little boy like you. Besides, I don't like either of you talking to strangers, you know."

"He is not a stranger. He is a friend. I just know it!"

Gabriella relented. "Okay, let's go and see the fountain then. Tomorrow." She'd be there to make sure the boys were safe. "I will ask Dad to join us. His university is just two blocks away. And we can all stop and grab something to eat at the coffee shop afterward."

The next day, Gabriella took her car keys and texted Jonas to ask him to join them at the fountain. As she opened the car door, she remembered her favorite phrase: "What is life but a dream?" She smiled to herself. Lewis Carroll's words. Her motto. How could she deny her boys their childhood wishes?

She pulled up to the school, and once both boys got into the car, she told them, "Seatbelts on. We're going to the fountain."

André sat behind the driver's seat, his favorite place. He took a deep breath, smiled at his brother sitting next to him, and looked out of the window. Cloudy dragons floated freely in the sky. The time had come to meet a good, new friend.

THOMAS'S JOURNAL

SIX PROVOKING QUESTIONS

Can you see with your eyes closed?

Can you hear with fingertips?

Can you smell without breathing?

Can you taste without eating?

Can you feel without touching?

Can you sense all the senses without making any sense?

THE FOUNTAIN

Thomas's black suit, black hat, and white shirt reflected on the taxi window as he left the cab. His style was personal—the old black hat had belonged to his father, and he'd found the suit in a charity shop. It was love at first sight; he had to have it.

Thomas walked toward the center of the square in Sao Paulo delighted to find his favorite bench, right in front of the fountain, free. He interpreted the empty seat as an invitation and sat right in the middle, opened his suitcase, and took out his journal. He loved sitting and listening to the sprinkling water and its fresh, dripping sounds, the echoes of children's laughter and the birds singing on the tree branches. Thomas took off his hat, closed his eyes, and let the sun's rays caress his face. Should he open his journal and write a few words? Or should he just take out his guitar and play a bit? So many questions, but instead of answering them, he sat there and enjoyed the pleasantness of it all, allowing himself to become a blank page, words floating in the air and musical notes erupting from his own inner spring.

Thomas pushed his hair back and put on his hat. In the quiet contemplation, he'd dozed off, the sun dipping behind the gray clouds that now covered the sky. The wind had picked up too, and, without warning, it blew the hat from his head.

"Dad's hat? Oh, no!"

Heads turned to watch Thomas, guitar on his back, journal in his hands, running madly in pursuit of the hat. The black hat seemed to have a mind of his own, longing for freedom, flying up and down before finally landing in the lap of a small boy who'd sat on Thomas's bench.

The child immediately put the hat on his head of curly hair, and Thomas hesitated. How could he take it away from the boy? The hat was his toy. And one should never ever take a toy out of a child's hand. Thomas looked around; should he give up his hat?

Thomas thought about his father. He missed him so much, the hat his only remaining connection. He placed his guitar back in its case before looking back at the child. He opened his mouth ready to ask for it back, but the child started laughing and caressing his guitar case. Thomas hesitated once more. The boy looked up.

"Who are you?"

"My name's Thomas."

"This belongs to you," the boy said as he handed the hat back.

Thomas graciously accepted and placed the hat firmly on his head. The little boy looked at the guitar case and then the notebook Thomas held at his side. "Are you a writer?"

Another smaller boy approached. "Are you a musician?" he asked, a look of awe on his face.

"I can play for you, kids, if that's what you want!" Thomas said, reaching to open his guitar case. In doing so, he dropped the journal on the ground. He always kept small notes and Post-its inside it, along with loose pages. They contained all his ideas for the future, dreams, and plans. When the journal landed, the loose pages and notes scattered, encouraged by the wind, flying around the square.

Thomas left the guitar with the boys and ran after his papers. Some people tried to help him; others just laughed. They could not see all the free musical beings flying around above their heads. The older of the two boys jumped up to help Thomas and began to hum a tune, a unique melody Thomas knew so well. He paused. How could this boy hum the melody? Thomas had composed it himself. He was about to ask him when the wind suddenly stilled.

Thomas looked around and realized the other benches were now crowded. People were staring at him, probably expecting him to play.

A girl with long, dark hair and large eyes smiled at him. She was wearing hand-crafted sandals and a white cotton dress with colorful beads around her neck. She, too, looked around before nodding, confirming that he play his music. He knew, instinctively, she belonged to the forest people.

Thomas stared at her, startled when the older boy handed him a shining object—a homemade toy of some sort. An exquisite little creature. The head of a dragon, the body of a fat cat, and the tail of a horse. Most unusual. The little boy certainly liked to create things. An inventor in the making.

Thomas sat on the ground, his inner child taking over. "Who are you? I want to thank you properly."

"I am André, and this is my brother Miguel," he said, pointing to the other small boy who'd helped chase the pages.

"This is our cat dragon, and we'd like you to have it."

Feeling deeply grateful and boyishly happy, Thomas held the toy to his heart. Somehow, he felt whole. He looked back at the smiling forest girl, gratitude spreading throughout his body, although he didn't know why. He nodded, stood up, and took his seat. With his guitar, he started to play.

THOMAS'S JOURNAL

THE RAIN DANCES
TO THE CLOUDS' WISHES
SO SKIES CAN DREAM.

Ideas for Songs.

THOMAS'S JOURNAL

A Puzzle

If something already beautiful increases in beauty, can it still be so?

If something horrible becomes something else, can it still be so?

Is there ugliness in perfect beauty?

Is there beauty in perfect ugliness?

Can ugliness reach perfection?

THE SCRIPTWRITER

Gabriella loved scriptwriting for so many reasons. Not only could she turn her imagination into something "real" and make money out of it, but she also got to spend time with her kids. It often meant working late hours, but she didn't mind.

She sat on the bench by the fountain that afternoon, gazing at the sun's rays reflected on the water. She realized that all the good things in her life were brought about by her children, André and Manuel. Her perception and intuition enhanced after André's birth. Maybe learning the wordless communication between mother and child had helped her notice other people's bodies and faces more accurately. Unsaid words become so meaningful. It even improved her relationship with Jonas, the children's father. It changed her concept of elegance and order. She recalled André's messy bedroom and how it had become the coziest space in her house. When Miguel was born, magic happened. The boy quickly created this whole new world of unsaid needs and orders; his make-believe games took over her life and thoughts.

Sometimes the boys seemed to lead her to the best places. Just like now. How could they have guessed the fountain square was the best place to be on a summer afternoon?

As she opened her eyes again, she noticed the boys sitting beside a young musician—black hair, black hat, large smiling eyes, and a guitar case by his side. She also saw his notebook and pen. Was he a writer just like her? She'd definitely like to talk to him and listen to him. There was something about him, something inherently good that drew her attention.

A strong breeze scattered his loose pages, and her boys tried to help him recover them. A drawing flew by her, and Gabriella left the bench to pick it up. As she held the page, she saw the image of a cat dragon. *Unbelievable!* she thought, as memories of André telling her he needed to meet someone he had dreamt about at the square flooded her brain. The boys had built a weird toy that resembled a dragon with a cat head. She'd thought it an ugly thing, made from pieces of old, broken toys.

The man had smiled at her boys when they offered him their homemade dragon, and Gabriella knew for certain that he was indeed a very nice young man. When he started playing, she was immediately drawn in by the deep, enchanting music that seemed to unveil secret realms to her. As she looked at the people gathered around to listen, she imagined she could sense their souls.

Seated on one of the surrounding benches, she spotted a tall man, in a sophisticated suit with white neatly trimmed hair and glasses. He raised his chin slightly as if to convey superiority. Next to him stood a well-dressed girl. She was slim with delicate hands and a beautiful profile. She also lifted her chin, and Gabriella guessed they were father and daughter.

There was something familiar about the girl, and it took a moment for Gabriella to remember who she was. Then she realized, the girl was a social media celebrity. Her father also seemed familiar, and Gabriella wondered if the young musician had invited them to hear him play. But why would they come? They didn't look like the type of people who would spend time near the fountain or enjoy an afternoon of free music. No, they looked like they would be more at home at VIP musical events with first-class seats and exclusive this and that. What on earth could they want with the young man?

Her thoughts were tainted by a subtle sense of mistrust. They were obviously very wealthy, and she'd known so many people like them—housed in wonderful manors yet filled with boredom, emotional misery, and empty souls. *Money can't buy me love*, she thought, laughing as she remembered the words of the old Beatles' song.

As a skilled scriptwriter, Gabriella started silently asking questions about the musician. When she saw him smile at the father and daughter, inexplicable doubts overcame her. Were these people the musician's friends? She hoped not. Her boys displayed so much affection for the young man, and she couldn't bear to see them disappointed. Her boys were always great at judging people's characters, and they liked him. She couldn't understand, then, why he would enjoy being surrounded by people who clearly acted as if they were above everyone else.

Soul thieves . . . they move so swiftly, so skilled at poisoning shiny minds. Could the musician sense how dangerous they could actually be? Gabriella's mind raced as she scanned the crowd, looking for more danger. Her eyes landed on a beautiful young girl sitting on the bench next to her. The girl was entranced by the musician. Most of the people around the fountain had their eyes closed, and their faces held half-smiles. Not this girl. She kept her eyes wide open. From the beads on her neck and wrist, and her plain cotton dress, Gabriella assumed she was of the forest people. This was the reason her gaze was unlike the others. She seemed to be deeply connected to the musician's gaze. It was as if they were having a dream-like conversation. Had they met before?

Pajé: Portuguese word originated from Tupi language. It designates a shaman who has the spiritual power of communicating with all sorts of visible or invisible beings. The living and the dead.

A seer, an herbalist, who can practice healing by the means of traditional sacred knowledge orally transmitted through several generations of forest dwellers.

THE RAIN CHILD

Popygua opened his hands and watched the shiny, round raindrops slide through his palms. He closed his eyes to enjoy their refreshing touch. He let his long, white hair be washed by the soft rain. He had so much to do before dawn. He had to collect the sacred leaves to make tea for a feverish little girl, and it would be a full moon that night.

After practicing his healing art at the praying house, Popygua sat by the riverbank and raised his eyes up to the sky, searching for wisdom.

He looked around him. He missed his beloved granddaughter Marlui. He longed to hear her laughter and soft steps, to see her smile that poured happiness into his soul. Maitê, the feverish little girl, would soon recover. Popygua knew that children got sick from time to time, but even so, he couldn't wait to see her playing in the trees again.

At first, worries invaded him as noisy, annoying flies trying to steal away his thoughts, but they soon gave way to a variety of emotions. Marlui was away in the city. She believed she could go to college and keep the forest in her heart. Popygua was not so sure about it, though. Marlui could see so many things. She understood the language of birds, snakes, monkeys, and all the forest dwellers. When she was but a little girl, she used to sit next to him during the ceremonies at the praying house. She could speak to their ancestors and quickly learn about the tales of wisdom, the healing herbs, and foretell things to come after watching birds fly across the sky. Marlui was a rain child.

The wind caressed his face, and he took a long, deep breath, letting all his thoughts leave him as he became one with the river. As a fish, now in the deep waters, he felt free. Then, he left the river. Beyond his own nature, words, and skies, Popygua became the void. Not a star nor a serpent, he was nothing but a human being. The healer opened his eyes and hands. Blue clouds against the horizon.

Then his spirit traveled over the timeless forest, and he could see a day to come. In his mind's eye, the old healer saw his grandchild sitting on a bench. He could hear echoes of beautiful music. Marlui was listening to songs played by a dark-haired young man. Popygua sat by the bench next to Marlui and enjoyed the music too. However, there seemed to be something very unusual about this man, as if he could sense Popygua's presence by Marlui's side. *How could that be?* Popygua listened to the music very carefully. The young man played his guitar in a very entrancing way. Popygua could hear the forest breathing through the instrument.

He opened his eyes, allowing the vision to fade. He felt puzzled. He and Marlui were used to having their spirits silently traveling together. This time, however, Marlui's musician friend somehow became part of the vision too, sensing his traveling spirit.

Popygua stood, thinking, *I must ask Marlui to bring this young man here to the forest. I want to find out about his music.*

THE CALLING

Thomas stopped playing and looked around. The square was crowded. It always came as a surprise to him whenever he realized the magnetic quality of his music. He had never meant to be a professional guitar player. He had picked up instruments in a bid to try and communicate with his secret sound beings. They always brought him such joy, especially in moments of sadness and desolation. When life was just fine, his happiness seemed intensified.

Just like now.

Thomas had decided to play by the fountain because of a calling he'd felt when he approached the square. As a young boy, his parents often took him to the fountain. His mother would buy him popcorn while his father would sit by his side and whistle classical tunes. They had both encouraged him to learn music, and being so young, he had the opportunity to learn from skilled teachers.

"Let's have a musical moment!" his father used to say. Then, he'd select a record from his beloved vinyl collection and play it. Thomas always enjoyed watching his father's gestures, his hands swinging through the air as if he were conducting an invisible orchestra. But that was long ago. Now they only met in dreams, and Thomas would wake to realize his father was gone. The pain was still unbearable.

Thomas had left home feeling a bit puzzled, his body invaded by an unsettling fear. He'd taken the trip to the square to try and push the uncanny sensation away, and it was only now that it was starting to make sense. The urge to leave the house and seek shelter outside hadn't made sense. His home was his shelter. As he played by the fountain and watched the audience enraptured in the music, a sense of calm washed over him. He stood up to thank his audience after they applauded. As he bowed, he was struck by the most beautiful eyes staring back at him. Mesmerized, he took off his hat to greet the girl. Who was she? He wanted to know her name. She was striking. Dark hair flowed down her back, and she wore a plain, white dress, open-toed sandals, and beads around her long, delicate neck.

He could have gazed at her for hours, merging with her dark eyes, but the audience asked for more music. Thomas lifted his guitar again and nodded in thanks to another young woman smiling at him.

"That's our mom!" the kids told him.

Thomas looked again. The three of them resembled each other. Before he started playing again, he heard one of the little boys say, "Gabriella. That's Mom's name. I am André, and he is Miguel."

The boy's voice mingled with the sounds of Thomas's strings as he closed his eyes and allowed the music to lead him once more. He let go of the memory of his parents and returned to his mind as vivid images began to take over.

THOMAS'S JOURNAL

ANCESTRAL WISDOM

Life flows as a river,

Feelings flow as water,

Clouds can hide the Sun's smile

Or the beauty of the shining Moon.

But the rain can bring life to Earth,

And an ocean can grow from a single raindrop.

FLYING DREAMS

The raindrops were larger and stronger when Marlui's gaze fell upon Thomas's flying drawing. She sensed her grandfather's presence, as well as the rain spirits. *Grandpa must be worried. I should go back home now!* The thought evaporated just as quickly as she found herself entranced by the strange beauty of the magical beings on the pages of the notebook." Are these drawings yours? Are you an artist? These are so beautiful!" she said as she touched the drawings in Thomas's notebook.

He stared for a moment before taking a sip of water. He smiled. "Are they really mine? I don't know. Sometimes I think I belong to them and not the other way around . . ."

Marlui nodded.

Thomas continued, "Art is an infinite ocean. I mean, the timeless space forever moving, becoming things like clouds, raindrops . . . and it feeds my soul, and I can become a teardrop because sometimes I cry while I am drawing, but I can also feel hungry. It depends . . ."

"Ah! You sound just like my grandfather," said Marlui, her eyes wide with surprise.

Thomas stared at the tall, old tree by the bench and whispered to her. "I can see your grandfather's face. He has long, white hair, piercing dark eyes. How long have you been away from home? He seems so worried about you."

Marlui's mouth hung open. She didn't know how to reply.

She'd never witnessed such power of perception among any of the people she met in town.

"Where do you live?" Thomas asked.

Marlui remained quiet.

"Am I being rude? Words just came out of my mouth! Sorry! I don't know what got ahold of me."

Marlui hesitated. "I just thought about him, my grandpa, I mean . . . funny. Yes, he must be upset. I should have been home by now, to help him collect the leaves for healing. He was taking care of a feverish girl when I left."

"Wow! I guessed right! Is your grandpa a healer? What's his name?" Thomas was struggling to keep the words in.

Marlui laughed. "Let me introduce myself to you first. I am Marlui. My grandfather is Popygua. We live by the lake, in the reserved area, near the forest on the way to the shore. How did you do that? How were you able to see his face? How can you talk as if you belong to and understand our ancient tradition?"

Thomas smiled, pride rising inside. It was the first time his perceptions hadn't been mistaken for craziness. There was something familiar and welcoming about the girl, and he found it so easy to confess his inner thoughts. "I don't know how I do it. I have always had visions, ever since I was a little boy. But I have never shared them. I was never sure if I could do that. To be honest, it feels so good to be able to say them out loud. Now, it is your turn! Please, tell me more about your ancient traditions."

Marlui giggled. It amused her to see the young man so awkwardly happy.

Thomas giggled along with her before settling himself again. "Okay! Okay, so, you are Marlui, the granddaughter of a powerful forest healer. Nice to meet you. My name is Thomas."

"My grandfather speaks as you do. He says his healing power

doesn't belong to him at all. It flows from the earth; his hands and herbs are mere tools. He says he belongs to the earth and calls himself an earth keeper."

"Really? Wow. This is an unusual conversation to be having, but I'd like to show you something." Thomas opened his small notebook to a page in the middle.

Marlui looked down and read.

GOLDEN RULE

Every keeper must eventually tear themselves away from the treasures they have been assigned to keep. Emptiness will lead to fulfillment, and a time for change will come. Living is changing.

VERA

*"'Tis true without lying, certain and most true
That which is below is like that which is above
and that which is above is like that which is below
to do the miracle of the one thing"*
—The Emerald Tablet, Hermes Trismegistus

Sitting on the bench on that sunny afternoon, Vera closed her eyes to truly enjoy the melodies being played by the young musician. As she allowed herself to be swept away by the relaxing beauty of the moment, the strange words from *The Emerald Tablet* floated across her mind. It was her mother's favorite ancient text. Its mysterious sentences that made no sense to her but were cherished by her mother. Cosmic, ancient laws puzzled her, and it was one of the reasons why she'd decided to go to law school and leave her mother's teachings aside. Her mother, Claire, had come from France and brought with her a large library of books on metaphysics and ancient philosophy. As a teenager, Vera would spend hours trying to decipher the hidden meanings of the cosmic poetry. It was useless, though. None of it ever made sense. Her mother appreciated her efforts and rewarded her with snacks. Vera could still recall the smell of the tea and cake.

Vera wondered if the musician knew how evocative his sounds were. How he had become so skilled. He seemed so young. At that moment, Vera realized that she felt younger as she listened. She watched the children laughing and the adults watching him with their eyes closed. Teenage girls danced to the music. What a gift it was. She'd left the university that day feeling overwhelmed by mounting assignments and the growing tension among her students, tests, tight schedules, and so on. Why had she ever chosen law school? The answer was clear. Unlike her mother, who only cared about the hidden, secret laws of the universe, Vera wanted to make a difference. She believed in social justice, improving people's lives, and fighting for human rights.

Her gaze fell on the beautiful young girl sitting on the bench next to her. She was of the forest people. Vera knew this from her clothes, and she smiled. There was a soothing quality to the girl.

Listening to the musician, she tapped into the myriad of memories she'd held onto. She felt blessed for the glimpses she'd had into ancient lives—the medieval texts she'd read so many years ago still imprinted on her mind.

> *All things in all universes move according to law, and the law which regulates the movement of the planets is no more immutable than the law which regulates the material expressions of human beings. The great aim of the mystery schools of all ages has been to reveal the workings of the law which connects people to the great search for light, life, and love.*

The music stopped. People clapped and thanked the musician for his gift. Vera clapped as well, gratitude filling her heart. The young man stood, stared at her, and bowed. Vera smiled back and looked around her. She recognized Gabriella, her colleague Jonas's beautiful wife, scribbling in a notebook. There were children playing with strange toys and having so much fun. A couple of ladies held each other, moved by the sound and beauty. The forest girl with the simple white dress looked toward the clouds. For a brief moment, Vera thought that this girl knew the hidden cosmic mysteries, or how to search for them, as Vera had once done at that age.

Vera's smile spread across her lips, something she had not done for quite some time. The girl smiled back as if they were lifelong friends. Vera spotted her colleague, Dr. Alonso. He was one of the most renowned teachers and researchers at the university. She didn't feel like greeting him. She resented his presence at that moment, as if he'd invaded her private space. He stood in his suit and elegant shoes, his air of superiority foreign among such a wonderful crowd. *Why is he here?* She didn't dare ask.

She watched as Dr. Alonso walked toward the musician and found herself doing the same. As she approached, she saw Dr. Alonso give the young man his card. She cleared her throat. "Dr. Alonso! What a surprise!"

"The famous Dr. Vera Barroso! I never expected to meet you here, away from your students, just listening to this stunning music!"

Vera felt guilty for having felt so uncomfortable about Dr. Alonso being there. He greeted her so cheerfully.

"Let me introduce you to my daughter, Dora!" he said as a sophisticated girl approached them.

Just as Vera turned to greet Dora, the musician spoke. "Hello, nice to meet you all. I am Thomas! Thank you for sharing your time with me and my music."

As people heard his name, another round of applause spread around the square, the full crowd now celebrating his music. Thomas returned to his bench, took his guitar, waited for a moment, as if trying to reconnect with his musical self, and started to play once more.

GABRIELLA

Gabriella hadn't expected to find a new story. She'd left home to please the boys and expected an afternoon of relaxation. Not that chasing stories ever made her nervous or upset—just the opposite. Gabriella loved chasing stories. She loved trying to focus and reason according to her own set of secret rules. She loved trying to guess what people's lives were like, their biographies, and their motives. In order to chase a good story, Gabriella relied on her vivid imagination, and it was in the act of finding out what to write about that she became aware of the exact moment when new words presented themselves. She had to be there and sense how to seize them.

On that specific afternoon, Gabriella had taken her notebook out. It was a habit. Nothing could be more predictable or uneventful than spending a summer afternoon by the fountain downtown. She'd been wrong. As the music mesmerized and entranced her, new stories invaded her mind. Music always seemed to trigger her ideas, but she also found herself puzzled by the audience the musician had attracted. Such an unusual crowd.

"Is this musician the friend you dreamt about?" she asked André.

"Yes, of course!" André replied matter-of-factly.

Gabriella wanted to ask him how he could have dreamt about someone he'd never seen before. How bizarre it was to actually meet them the following day. She knew it was useless. André would have taken his time to tell her all about this beautiful, senseless dream. He would have spoken nonstop, and she would still be clueless. Instead, she tried to observe the people, watching how they too were entranced by the music.

"Thomas."

She heard the musician introduce himself to the tall, handsome, well-dressed man. He looked to be in his seventies and was accompanied by a much younger woman. Father and daughter, Gabrielle surmised, their resemblance so obvious not only in their facial expressions but in their strong sense of self. They both wore designer clothes and had a slightly arrogant way as they spoke with the young man. They appeared privileged.

Gabriella opened her notebook and wrote down *Nothing is ever as it seems to be.* She gave up on trying to play a detective and gather information about these people's lives. Instead, she focused on the impressions they generated in her mind. She heard the father and daughter introduce themselves as Dr. Alonso and Dora.

"Gabriella!"

Jonas, her beloved husband, came running toward her and the kids. He stopped to greet Dr. Alonso, and she realized they must be colleagues. She couldn't remember Jonas mentioning him before, and she thought it odd since he loved to talk about his daily routine. She looked at Dr. Alonso, ready to introduce herself. He didn't greet her, or even smile, and it left her a little uncomfortable. *Strange.* He turned to his daughter and said something Gabriella didn't catch. Dora glared at her, as if warning her not to intrude. Gabriella shrank back. Was she overreacting? Was it her sensitivity as a writer? Had she imagined the brush-off, or were they really trying to control the situation and keep the musician focused on them?

Gabriella decided it didn't matter. She didn't particularly like either of them, but she could be totally wrong.

"Mom! Dad is here!" screamed André.

Pulled from her thoughts, Gabriella looked at Jonas and realized that even after ten years of living together, she still felt immense joy in his presence. The musician waved at her, and she left her seat. She kissed Jonas and greeted the young musician. "Your music has made me dream. Thank you!

Thomas showed her the little cat dragon. "Your boys have given me such a stunning toy! Can I really accept this gift?"

"Absolutely!" said Jonas.

Gabriella nodded and smiled at Thomas. She was so proud of her boys and their creativity and generosity toward the young musician.

Thomas sat back on his bench and dedicated the beautiful song to the boys and all the other children who had answered the magical call of his music. Gabriella closed her journal, and then her eyes, and allowed herself to cross the enchanted gates of timeless lands.

INSTANT FRIENDSHIPS

"Were you writing a story while I played?" asked Thomas. Gabriella smiled, feeling like a child who was caught in the act. "Yes, indeed!"

Thomas was holding the cat-dragon toy while he continued to ask her all sorts of questions. He moved from his bench to theirs, wanting to be closer to his new friends. "Are you a professional writer, I mean, a real author? Or are you someone like me, who just enjoys seizing the day through words?"

Gabriella enjoyed his instant friendship and made room for him by her side. "I'm a professional scriptwriter, but I also like to write at random. I keep journals, notes scattered all over our house. Here . . ." She grabbed a piece of paper from her pocketbook and handed it to him. "Take my card."

Thomas took it and placed it in his pocket whilst retrieving one of his own. "Will you take my card too? Maybe we could get together to talk about writing styles sometime?"

Gabriella smiled at him as Jonas sat beside them. Jonas shook Thomas's hand. "Gabriella is a true writer. You should see her, Thomas. Whenever she starts writing, I get the feeling she's hearing voices from outer space. I mean, she looks so entranced, I have a hard time believing she is really inventing. It wouldn't surprise me if she was downloading narratives from some unseen dimension only she has access to."

"Don't be dramatic," Gabriella protested.

"I understand what he means," said Thomas. "People tend to experience strange sensations when they watch me play. They keep asking me where my inspiration comes from, and the only answer I can give is that I don't really know."

The trio laughed, amazed at how comfortable they felt with each other.

"Here, Thomas, take my card too," said Jonas. "I teach law at the nearby university."

The conversation was interrupted.

"Can I sit with you?" Marlui asked as she stood in front of them.

Thomas immediately made space for her to sit on the bench. André and Manuel came closer too, intrigued by the young woman who'd joined them. "Are you from the forest?" André asked, reaching up to touch her colorful necklace. "I have seen people wearing necklaces and earrings like yours in my schoolbooks."

"It shouldn't just be from books that you recognize my people's jewelry," Marlui said. "You should come and visit us in the forest sometime." She smiled at André before continuing. "I am Marlui and I belong to the forest community. My grandfather would love for you to visit." She turned directly to Thomas. "Please come and visit us too. I think you'd really enjoy it."

Before anyone could replay, Dora appeared. "May I join you?" She didn't wait for a response and stood right in front of Thomas, staring into his eyes and ignoring everyone else. She pointed at her father. "Thomas, my father wants to exchange words with you."

Jonas immediately stood in front of Thomas in a seemingly protective manner. "Hello, there, Alonso! Nice to meet a colleague here at the fountain! Are you done teaching your classes today?"

Dr. Alonso ignored his question and moved toward Thomas, who had risen from his seat to shake the professor's hand. "Nice to meet you, sir. My father was also a professor, an architect that taught at the university."

Dr. Alonso stepped in close to Thomas and tapped him on the shoulder. "Glad to hear that, son. I am sure he must be very proud of you. Dora has shown me your site, and I have listened to your music, but seeing you live has been a true privilege indeed."

Thomas looked away. "My father passed away when I was still a boy. He didn't live long enough to see me become a musician." He cleared his throat, realizing the melancholy in his voice. "But, of course, I heard music from the cradle. My mother played the piano, and my father, the violin. She has passed too."

Marlui rose from her seat. All she wanted to do was hug Thomas. She too understood the meaning of loss and pain, but Dr. Alonso somehow anticipated her intervention. He moved Thomas to the side, guarding the young musician with his arm. Marlui tried to approach Thomas again, but Dora intercepted her, smiling sweetly. Marlui was puzzled by the girl's subtle animosity, the contrast between her beauty and her rude gesture. She didn't know what to say, or how to act. Marlui's hesitation lasted long enough for Dr. Alonso to do whatever it was he intended.

"May I invite you to dinner, Thomas? I will not take no for an answer, young man. I must show you my collection of medieval musical instruments. I am sure you will be delighted. Why not come with us now? My car is parked nearby."

Jonas, sensing Marlui's unease and not quite understanding what Dr. Alonso was up to, stood up. "I'm really interested in your research, Dr. Alonso. Perhaps I could pay you a visit as well."

Vera appeared by Jonas. She'd been listening to what was going on. "I'd certainly enjoy visiting and seeing your collection as well, Dr. Alonso."

Dr. Alonso smirked. "Dear friends, I am so sorry I'm taking

this amazing young musician away from you, and I appreciate you all wanting to visit. Don't worry my daughter and I will be in touch with you soon. Perhaps we could have a large musical gathering soon. I'd love the pleasure of your company."

To everyone's dismay, Thomas picked up his guitar and turned to Dr. Alonso. "I accept your invitation. I'd love to see your collection of historical instruments. Shall we go now?"

The boys looked forlorn as they hugged Thomas's legs. Marlui leaned forward and kissed him gently on the cheek. Gabriella hugged him tight. Jonas was the last to say goodbye. "Thomas, you have my number. Call me anytime at all."

Dora grinned triumphantly as she took Thomas's arm and led him to their car. Dr. Alonso waved goodbye to all of them and quickly moved out of the square.

Gabriella turned to her new friends. "I must say, I don't feel comfortable with all that. There is something so uncanny about this man." She turned to Jonas. "Who is this Dr. Alonso person?"

Jonas scratched his chin. "He does have a strange reputation. I mean, apparently, he researches myths, besides teaching law at the university. I've always felt there was something off about him. It is hard to explain. There have been lots of rumors."

"Oh, dear," whispered Gabriella, conscious of the boys. "I can't believe this. I hate it when I get a bad feeling about someone, and it proves to be spot on."

"We want to listen to Thomas again," said little André.

"Did he say when he was going to play again?" asked Vera. "Maybe he will be back to the square soon."

"How about we meet here again, tomorrow, just in case?" suggested Marlui. "I really want to meet Thomas once more. As he played, I got the feeling I needed to take him to speak to my grandpa."

Gabriella smiled. Marlui was as interesting as she had imagined.

"Feelings?" asked Vera, a bit suspicious. "Is it how you make your decisions? Based upon feelings, hunches?"

Marlui stared at her calmly but said nothing.

Jonas shook his head. "I must say, I got an uncanny feeling when I realized this young man, who is so gifted and sensitive and who played with our kids and shared his music so generously, was leaving with Alonso and his daughter. It didn't seem right or natural. I wish we'd invited him and all of you to supper instead." He smiled then. "His music has brought us all together, you know."

"Listen, how about we meet again in this square, tomorrow, at this time?" insisted Marlui. "Has Thomas left his phone number with any of you?"

"Yes!" said Gabriella. "He gave me his card. Should I text him?"

"Thomas also has my number. If something weird happens, I mean . . ." Jonas trailed off.

"I gave him my card as well," Gabriella said. She turned to André. "Do you think your friend will be here tomorrow?"

André smiled, looked down, and then shook his head. "Well, maybe I will dream about him tonight."

Vera stood up. "I know I'm not a dreamy child, or a sensitive young lady like you, Marlui, but what Jonas and I could do is to ask around and see if your colleagues can tell us any more about Dr. Alonso. Then, of course, we can meet again and chat. Anyway, let's just hope for now that Thomas will be here tomorrow. I'd certainly love to listen to him again."

"I'll look him up on social media," said Gabriella. "And, of course, I agree with you. We have never seen each other before, but we are really beginning to sound like a team."

"Yes, it sounds like a good plan," said Jonas.

"Yes!" said André and Manuel at the same time, just a few seconds before light rain fell on the square again. People scattered and went wherever it was they had to be.

EL DESDICHADO

By Gérard de Nerval

Je suis le Ténébreux, – le Veuf, – l'Inconsolé,
Le Prince d'Aquitaine à la Tour abolie :
Ma seule *Etoile* est morte, – et mon luth constellé
Porte le *Soleil noir* de la *Mélancolie*.

Dans la nuit du Tombeau, Toi qui m'as consolé,
Rends-moi le Pausilippe et la mer d'Italie,
La *fleur* qui plaisait tant à mon cœur désolé,
Et la treille où le Pampre à la Rose s'allie.

Suis-je Amour ou Phébus ?… Lusignan ou Biron?
Mon front est rouge encore du baiser de la Reine;
J'ai rêvé dans la Grotte où nage la sirène…

Et j'ai deux fois vainqueur traversé l'Achéron :
Modulant tour à tour sur la lyre d'Orphée
Les soupirs de la Sainte et les cris de la Fée.

THOMAS'S JOURNAL

I am a street-walking charcoal with a heart full of songs

The Duke of Aquitaine who tortures tertulias 'till boredom.

My lonesome star unstuck has gone,

A black hole from the sun—a star was born.

But is there any sanctuary in that sunny tomb?

Biting me right in the core like a *dolce stil nuovo* song.

A flower is a flower, but it is only a word

Desolation row, wasted land, or horrific world

With its last fingered dawn, like that verse, so rose,

The pain in painting, the poem in Poe

Hölderlin sung his red words

A kino-prose, a nightmare that roars

Eye to eye, ace to ace, a mirror of horrors

I've been an ape on Sundays, a moron in love

A lyre elsewhere on a journey with no end

A sign in crisis, the trance of a saint,

Fire to fire, a criticism of breath, much worse.

MUSES AND GODS

"Orpheus, the strongest musician of Greek mythology, I am thinking in terms of poetical power, my friend . . . Of course, according to mythology researchers, ancient bards and troubadours were also great masters, especially the Celtic Taliesin, but I must say the symbolism of his myth contains so many levels of meaning . . . Can you picture yourself as someone who was the true son of Calliope, the muse of music?"

Dr. Alonso asked Thomas some rhetorical questions left unanswered. Thomas could not concentrate on his long monologue.

As the car crossed the tunnel, leaving downtown on the way to the countryside, Thomas looked through the back window. A strong sense of regret mingled with an uncanny fear inside him. *Why am I here with these people? Why didn't I stay with my new friends? Why did I leave Marlui? Such a lovely being.*

Several questions crossed his mind as he felt overwhelmed and somewhat hypnotized by Dora's beauty. Her father's commanding voice pulled him back to the present.

"Yes, my young man, I must say, you make me think of Orpheus, so talented, so powerful, yet defeated and lost. Why do you keep on looking back? Are you feeling as if you have left someone behind? Don't worry. You can always catch up with your friends. All you have to do is to go back and play at the square." Dr. Alonso nodded at Dora. "Now, Thomas, we have a very special opportunity for you, a once-in-a-lifetime opportunity. Why don't you make yourself comfortable for now and prepare for the surprises that await in my home?"

Thomas couldn't really relate to Dr. Alonso's enthusiasm. A strong mistrust overtook him, and he felt like he'd been kidnapped. Dora turned around to face him, taking one of his hands in hers and stroking his hair with the other. She smiled seductively, and her strong gaze mesmerized him.

"You know the story of Orpheus, don't you, Thomas? Father is so right about it. What a timeless myth. I must confess, I can also connect you to my image of Orpheus," Dora said.

Thomas took a deep breath, trying to summon the courage to ask them to stop the car, to pull over and let him out. Sitting by his side on the back seat, Dora acted as if they had been longtime lovers. Dora's hands in his hair frightened him and stirred an attraction inside him that left him speechless. Her gestures, as she approached him in the car, seemed so natural and spontaneous; Thomas just could not avert them. He didn't want to hurt their feelings. Everything about them seemed genuine their smart clothes, well-spoken voices, gestures, and their self-confidence. He remembered the casual, suave way they had persuaded him to leave his friendly audience in the square. Dora's soft yet intense eyes fixed on him. They acted as if they belonged to some exclusive Olympic realm. But in all this, they wanted to share the space with him. Why?

Thomas knew Orpheus's myth by heart—the magic musician, the beautiful young singer, the poet that played his lyre, all the animals who followed him to listen to his songs and all the trees that danced to his tunes. When the Argonauts were crossing the sea assaulted by a ferocious storm, Orpheus's music appeased not only the ship's crew but also the sea, chasing away the clouds in the sky.

Dr. Alonso broke through his thoughts. "I am sorry if I have offended you, young man. I am sure you know the Orpheus myth by heart."

The car exited the tunnel, and Thomas watched the world whizz by. He cleared his throat. "Oh, yes, I do know the myth. I have mixed feelings about it. Love and hate. I have been obsessed with it for years now. Not because I like it, just the opposite . . ."

"This is fabulous! A young, contemporary Orpheus who hates his own narrative . . . very interesting, indeed," said Dr. Alonso, his eyes staring at the road ahead.

Dora looked across at Thomas, reaching to stroke his hair again, but he had turned his head away.

"Is the road always so silent?" he asked her, just to make conversation.

"Silent? I don't understand. It is so noisy! Can't you hear the car horns?"

He didn't like the way she smiled at him and tried to hide the strange feelings creeping in. He turned his gaze to the window, instinctively looking for his musical beings, trying to listen to them, to seize their subtle movements. Drops of rain began to fall on the window. But there was nothing.

No secret sounds.

His musical companions were nowhere to be seen, nor heard.

Thomas had never felt so alone.

THOMAS'S JOURNAL

When I think in my bedroom,

Where, unfortunately,

I know no one can enter,

Not a brother, nor an uncle,

All my limbs,

All my fingers,

All my nails,

Cannot stop trembling,

Cannot stop shaking,

And as a feverish child,

I deeply fear,

No longer being so close to your soul.

THE TROUBADOUR

Half an hour had passed, but Thomas still couldn't relax. Tired, he told Dora he wanted to take a quick nap before dinner, but when he found himself lying on the king-size bed in the huge and well-furnished guest room at Dr. Alonso's country manor, he couldn't sleep. He felt restless. It had been such a long day—all afternoon playing by the fountain, the unexpected car trip to the countryside, with people he had never seen before . . .

He looked at his guitar. He always kept it near him, a sort of talisman companion. He reached out his hand to hold the instrument, but he couldn't touch it. Usually, his secret creatures of sound would play on the chords, soothing him until he would fall asleep.

Thomas walked up to the window and opened it, looking for stars, but all he could see was sheer darkness. As he closed his eyes, recent scenes invaded his thoughts, so vivid that he felt his hands shaking upon the windowpane.

Dr. Alonso had parked the car in the driveway. A smiling, short, robust lady with curly hair in a tight bun, wearing a white apron, had offered to carry his guitar, which he refused. The three of them then walked through the elaborate hall; the medieval pictures, which were obviously genuine, hung on the towering walls. There was a collection of ancient, magical objects, including sacred ritual knives, enchanted stones, and handwritten journals in medieval French displayed in polished wood cabinets.

Dr. Alonso's face expressed his deep satisfaction as he felt Thomas's curiosity and awe. Alonso also sensed the mixed feelings displayed on Thomas's face as he took in his surroundings—the uncanny fascination, the discomfort, and his gaze back at the door as if he wanted to run from the place.

"Dinner will be served soon." A cook in lavish attire informed them.

Thomas was taken to the guest bedroom. He had expected to stay for dinner and go back home, but he didn't feel like refusing that implicit invitation to stay overnight. Everything seemed to have been arranged previously and he did not know how to react. He did not feel like upsetting his host. He entered the bathroom to wash his hands. He looked at the mirror. He almost didn't recognize his own face. All his life, he'd seen his musical beings floating around him, reflected in mirrors, windows, and even water glasses. He'd always greeted them with a smile and spent a moment listening to their melodious voices. Their company brought him great joy and gratitude and had been as natural as breathing. "This is the first time I see my face completely alone," he mumbled as a deep sadness spread. The vulnerability of being alone seemed to add new deep lines around his now hollow eyes. Thomas felt as if he had aged ten years in a couple of hours.

"Are you ready, my dear?"

The voice he heard was human, sexy, and commanding. Dora's voice. It broke his reverie. He dried his hands on the towel before opening the bedroom door, his mouth hanging open in surprise. "What is this?"

Dora stood before him with blonde, short hair, laughing at his surprise. "This is the real me," she said, taking his arm to lead him to the dining room.

She wore a flower dress that skimmed the middle of her thighs and golden sandals, her perfectly manicured toenails peeking out. Her forehead was covered by blonde bangs, and a provocative smile danced upon her lips. "You mean, you had a wig on before?"

"Yes, I did. I like to keep my real self-separate from my work as a digital influencer. And besides, I hate being recognized when I go shopping, and I have to shop for clothes and cosmetics all the time." She fluttered her eyelashes and pushed her hair behind her ears.

"Please, don't take this the wrong way, but I've never heard about you."

"Oh, that's all right. I am a fashion influencer, and you are a musician, two different planets, so to speak."

Thomas smiled at his own awkwardness. They entered the dining room; then they were interrupted by yet another stranger.

"Welcome to our house, my lovely troubadour. Dora tells me you are truly one of a kind." The lady, Dora's mother, he presumed, moved toward him, smiling, pushing her long golden hair behind her shoulders. "Thank you. You must be Dora's mother. You both look so alike."

"Yes, you can call me Margaret. Take a seat."

Thomas suddenly felt shy and out of place. He was once again regretting his decision to accept the invitation. He didn't know these people. He took his seat, Margaret sitting across from him.

"Dora informed me that you were surrounded by a nice crowd today. I'm delighted she managed to lure you to our home."

"Actually, you should thank Dad," Dora said. "He was the one who promised Thomas he'd show him a genuine, medieval lute."

Thomas hadn't noticed Dr. Alonso enter the room and only looked up as he joined in the conversation.

"Oh, I knew he'd come. The troubadour in him would never refuse the chance to meet such a legendary instrument. Am I right, Thomas?"

Thomas didn't get the chance to verbally answer, but his head moved back and forth while following the conversation.

"I wasn't sure if he would come, after all." Dora grinned at Thomas. "There was a beautiful forest girl who'd captured your attention. You looked quite entranced."

"A true forest girl?" asked Margaret. "A native girl? What was she doing downtown?"

Thomas didn't like the disdain he heard in Margaret's voice. He stared at the crystal glass by his hand. He really missed the subtle sounds that would always suggest what he should say or do. Speechless and forlorn, he sipped the mineral water to disguise the growing desire he felt to leave this place. He let the conversation wash over him, his eyes taking in the elaborate dining room. He shrugged his shoulders and nodded his head when appropriate. He had turned to look at Dr. Alonso when he saw it. The lute. It hung on the wall. It was beautiful; something in it drew him to it. He sighed, knowing he couldn't leave now. He had to stay.

"She is beautiful, isn't she?" Dr. Alonso said, following Thomas's gaze. "Be patient, young man. First, you need to relax and have a good time. Only then will you be ready for her."

Dinner was followed by the most delicious dessert, and as Thomas reached for a second serving of the chocolate cake, his mood changed. He no longer felt he'd made a mistake in accepting the invitation. These strange people no longer felt like a threat, either, unusual as they might be. The scented candles spread throughout the room elicited a combination of sensations and emotions. He was enjoying the delicious food and wine, the comfy furniture, sensual Dora, and the medieval music that seemed to reach in and seize his soul.

After dinner, he sat on a plush velvet sofa. Dora's perfume filled his nostrils, and he found himself laughing at Margaret's jokes. He drank coffee and listed to Dr. Alonso's travel stories from around the world. He felt cozy, comfortably numb, something he hadn't felt in quite some time.

After returning to his room, however, all the relaxing sensations evaporated, giving way to a series of shivers running up and down his spine. He noticed that dawn was breaking. He hadn't slept. He pulled back the covers. He had to sleep even if it meant hypnotizing himself into a dream state.

He thought of Marlui's face, her eyes shining with the soothing beauty of still waters. He sat upright. He couldn't sleep. His mind was too busy. He wondered where Marlui was now. Was she back in her community? Would she be walking among the trees at night? He longed to speak to her again, to be somewhere else. The sensation was so strong. Thomas cursed his own stupidity. Why had he allowed himself to be seduced into coming here? Why had it been so easy for them to persuade him to go with them? Why hadn't he done what he'd wanted to do, spend time in the company of the young woman he had wanted so much to connect with?

Marlui could see his creatures of sound—he just knew it. He'd watched as she stared at him playing, and he was sure she had the eyes that *saw* too. Not only his musical beings but all sorts of other mysterious things. But he had run away, left her. He'd allowed Dr. Alonso and Dora to persuade him into following them rather than choosing to follow his own truth. He thought of the lute just outside his bedroom, how it mesmerized him. He could forgive his foolish decisions for the chance to hold it, to play it. Perhaps it was all meant to happen. He knew Marlui was from the forest community. He'd be able to find his way back to her. "Maybe the lute was the true calling," he mumbled as he lay down and fell into a deep sleep.

Thomas looked at his cell phone. Seven a.m. It was a gray, cloudy morning, and the rain was splattering the curtains through the window he'd left open. He was about to get up and shut it when he heard a knock at the door.

"Thomas, are you awake?"

"Just a second." He rushed to the bathroom, threw water on his face, and brushed his hair, and then he put his clothes on and opened the door. Dora stood there, smiling. Her green eyes twinkled with mischief. He found himself challenged by her, contemplating her next move, and he found he enjoyed it. "You are still a blonde, then," he said, averting her gaze.

"Yeah, I got the feeling you liked my short, blonde hair better than my long chestnut wig."

"You've been playing pranks on me," Thomas said, feeling his face heat.

"I was just teasing you." Dora twirled a strand of her hair between her fingers as she maintained eye contact.

They'd barely reached the bottom of the stairs before Thomas was accosted again.

"Good morning, Thomas. Would you care to take a quick walk?" Margaret marched toward them and gripped Thomas's hand, leaving him no time to answer her question. She opened the door to the backyard and pulled him out. Thomas scanned quickly for an umbrella or raincoat, but there was nothing to protect him from the torrential downpour.

Once more dominated by someone else's will, Thomas followed Margaret, Dora close behind, doing his best to shield himself from the rain. The claps of thunder startled him, and his feet felt heavy as they made their way to a clearing surrounded by tall eucalyptus trees.

Focused on the heavy rain and the dark clouds that loomed overhead, Thomas lost his footing and tripped. As he plunged headfirst into the muddy hole, a sense of entrapment engulfed him. What had these two women planned for him? Why had they dragged him out in the rain? Why was he even here? The sticky mud clung to his clothes, his hands cold and wet as he tried to claw his way out. Margaret and Dora stood, watching him struggle, two pairs of green eyes glaring down at him, cold and sinister. Thomas opened his mouth to scream, only to have it filled with dirt. The mud blocked his throat so no sound could escape. All he could do was try to cover his face with his arms as the two venomous women proceeded to bury him alive.

Thomas bolted upright in the bed. Someone was knocking on the door. It wasn't real. It was a dream. He ran to the bathroom, feeling the sticky mud from his nightmare clinging to him. Pulling the handle for the shower, he jumped right in and allowed the water to wash over him. His body continued to shake and sweat beaded on his forehead.

The knocking continued. Thomas stepped out of the shower and wrapped a towel around his waist. "I will be out in a minute," he called as he willed his mind to settle.

"They are waiting for you, sir," the housekeeper called through the door.

Thomas dried himself off and reached for his clothes, all the while promising himself that he'd leave the house and its strange occupants immediately.

ORPHEUS

The myth of Orpheus dates back to ancient times.

The son of Oeagre and Calíope, the most powerful of all nine muses, Orpheus was an excellent singer, a musician, and a poet. He played the lyre. The instrument originally held seven chords, but Orpheus added two more. His music was so sublime—all animals followed him, all trees swayed to his voice, all plants blossomed, greeting him as he sang, and all men, no matter how hard their hearts were, became peacefully happy by listening to his songs.

Orpheus took part in the Argonaut's journey. During a tempest on the sea, he appeased the waves with his songs. When the sirens came to hypnotize men with their songs and make them dive into the deep sea, Orpheus sang and mesmerized the sirens so they could cross the waves unharmed.

Yet, his most popular narrative is related to his beautiful wife, the nymph named Euridice. She went out for a walk in the forest and was stalked by Aristeus, who wanted to kidnap her. As she fled from him, Euridice inadvertently stepped on a serpent and was bitten and died. Orpheus, inconsolable, went down to the underworld looking for her. Using his music as a magical shield, Orpheus seduced not only the dangerous creatures but the gods of the underworld: Hades and Persephone. They were both so touched by the beauty of Orpheus's music that Hades, the god of Death, and his wife, Persephone, decided to give the musician a chance to prove the depth of his love for Euridice. One single condition was imposed upon the young couple: Orpheus would be allowed to take the path back to light, followed by his wife; however, he couldn't turn back and look at her. The young musician was required to show his absolute trust in their love by avoiding looking at her, and she could only follow his footsteps.

Orpheus played his music while he headed out of hell. However, on his last steps, as their exit drew close, an uneasy dread overwhelmed him. Doubts clouded his mind. Was Euridice really following him? Were Hades and Persephone capable of keeping their word? Had he been deceived? What if Euridice had been kept in hell, and he had been misled, leaving her there forever?

He turned to look at his beloved, and in an instant, Euridice died, becoming trapped in hell for all of eternity.

Orpheus desperately tried to hold her and bring her back to life with the power of his music, but it was impossible. Orpheus was forced to return to the world of the living all alone.

All that was left for Orpheus was to sing about his lost love. His poignant music, now more beautiful than ever, broke the hearts of all women as they tried to make the musician love them and forget about Euridice. When they realized he would never be able to fully return their affection, the women became furious, and, eventually, Orpheus was beheaded.

After his death, his lyre was taken to the sky and became a constellation. Orpheus's soul was led to the Olympic fields where he started composing the most marvelous songs of love and happiness.

EARLY MORNING AT GABRIELLA'S

Gabriella read several versions of the myth of Orpheus. She decided to try and come up with a story that would highlight the relevance of his story for today's world. There were so many bright young musicians dying before their time. Music, she believed, was the most powerful of all the arts, which is why its priests, the children of Orpheus, are dangerous. Adored by their fanatical followers. Fans? It seemed so ambivalent. The power of music binding people yet blinding them to the vulnerable side of musicians. As generous as musicians seemed to be, constantly sharing their gifts, people just kept on asking for more and more. Sometimes stalking them as if they wanted to steal the secret of their creativity for themselves.

"My heroes died from overdose . . ." Gabriella hummed Cazuza's famous lyrics. She loved his songs; he was a young, beautiful son of Orpheus who died in his prime. Why are so many young musicians so naive? Heartbroken? Prey to modern-day vampires, wannabe celebrities, treacherous associates, and crazy fans? If music is the mother of all arts and such a powerful medium, why is it that the most talented artists seem unable to cope with their priesthood?

She left her dictionary of myths aside and reached for her purse. She'd placed the young musician's card inside. Holding it up, she was disappointed to see only his name on the front.

Thomas Felippe

Musician & composer

Flipping it over revealed a mobile number. She heaved a sigh of relief. She could call him, although she'd have to think of an excuse. He probably wouldn't understand her concern. She placed the card on the table. She couldn't figure out why she had an unsettling feeling about him. When Thomas played, he'd dominated the crowd, and then he just left with those shady people, Dr. Alonso and Dora. She'd never met Dr. Alonso before, but his attitude and demeanor had been enough to spur the dislike she felt. How had Thomas not seen his arrogance? Had he been blinded by Dora? She was beautiful, and she liked to flaunt it. What young man wouldn't have been taken in? Gabriella remembered what teen hormones were like and how easily it was to get distracted when lust took over.

Her mind raced, and she decided to write her feelings down. Perhaps, that way, she could make sense of them and see the reality of things, not the thriller her imagination conjured up. As she started to write, the words skipped. She couldn't find the storyline or the right metaphors that would transform the fear inside her into a narrative she could control. She knew she wouldn't be able to settle or calm her mind. She'd call him, which would make everything right. She'd tell him she wanted to interview him for the new piece on timeless Greek myth and how he might very well be a modern-day Orpheus.

ABSENCE

Vera arrived at the university half an hour before her class. She made her way to the teacher's office. The secretary was already there. "Has Dr. Alonso arrived? I would like to have a word with him."

The young woman looked up at her computer. "I'm afraid he called in sick. He won't be in today."

"Sick? Are you sure? I saw him and his daughter yesterday, and he seemed just fine."

"All I know is that he won't be coming into the university today. Would you like to leave him a message?"

"No, I will try to speak to him tomorrow." Vera huffed as she made her way to her class. What had gotten into her? Besides sitting on a bench to listen to music and talking to strangers she'd never met before, she'd actually broken her routine, and it was so out of character. What puzzled her most was the young musician and why he'd evoked such worry in her. What was it about him? She hardly knew him, and here she was worried about his well-being. She might never see him again, and it was so unlike her to interfere in people's affairs. With her mind made up, she decided it was best to focus on the day ahead and go back to being her normal self.

After class, exhausted from the constant churning of her mind, she decided to call it a day and go home and mark student papers. She had so much work to do. She'd just stepped out of the classroom when she heard her name. She turned to see Jonas Santos, her favorite colleague, approaching.

"Vera! So great to see you again. How are you feeling after the excitement at the fountain?"

Vera stopped and greeted him with a kiss on the cheek. She didn't get to answer his questions. Jonas, being Jonas, kept talking.

"I didn't think you had classes today. Have you changed your schedule? Great to see you again. Have you time for a coffee?"

"I was just about to leave, papers to mark," Vera said, motioning to the bundle of papers in her arms. "I'm sure I have time for a coffee, though."

Vera and Jonas chatted about mundane school stuff as they made their way to the coffee shop. As she sat on the stool, sipping the dark and much-needed liquid, she couldn't stop thinking about what had transpired at the fountain. "Jonas, what do you really think about Dr. Alonso? I want you to tell me everything you know. Something isn't sitting right with me."

"Well, yesterday, at the park . . . I'm not sure about you, but I felt that Dr. Alonso and his lovely socialite daughter were a little out of place. I'm still trying to figure out why they were there. It's unlike them to socialize with those below them. I've never seen him there before, and I did wonder if they orchestrated the whole thing, meeting Thomas, you know." He paused to reach for his coffee.

Vera looked around before leaning in closer. "I was quite confused about the whole thing myself. For Thomas to just leave and follow them. I'm a very skeptical woman but . . ." She shook her head. "My mother was a mystic, and I know that if she were still alive, she'd tell me Thomas had been hypnotized or coerced in some mystical way into following them."

"I know what you mean. There's something off about everything, and there's definitely something off about Dr. Alonso.

I just can't work out what it is."

"I know. And like I said, I don't actually believe in intuition, or this entire esoteric mumbo jumbo, but I really did feel something was wrong, like he was a predator who had managed to get his claws into his prey."

"Well, all I know," said Jonas, looking around nervously, "is that I had this very bright young student called Rafael who was also taking Dr. Alonso's classes. He was a sensitive fellow and truly creative. He could draw, write, and was a skilled piano player. One day, he told me he had been invited to Dr. Alonso's house. The next thing I know, he's infatuated with Alonso's daughter, Dora. Couldn't stop talking about her. I think they even became a couple. The thing is, he changed after that. He lost weight, he couldn't focus, and he seemed sick. I even thought for a moment that he was drinking heavily or taking substances. When I questioned him about it, he told me he'd just gotten the flu." Jonas peered behind him again, making sure no one could hear their conversation. "I met him in here sometime later, and as I greeted him, he fell into my arms and sobbed like a baby. I took him outside into the garden to find out what had happened. He kept on saying, over and over again, that his gift had been taken away, that he could no longer play. He said Dora dismissed him as soon as he lost his talent."

"That is so strange. How can someone's talents be taken away?"

"Exactly!" said Jonas. "I couldn't believe it. The poor boy—his whole body was shaking like he had withdrawal symptoms. He was mumbling and talking about things I couldn't understand. One thing I do remember, though, is him saying he had taken part in some kind of ritual. Apparently, it all started very beautifully. He was surrounded by beautiful people. He played his piano, performing for a small, private, elite group. That same night, he made love to Dora. He was feeling on top of the world. He was sure he had been chosen to be among the best, and said he felt like royalty."

"Why was he so upset then?" asked Vera.

"Have you ever thought about it, Vera, being on top of the world? I'd hate it. As a friend of mine always says, '*exclusive* means *excluding*, not blending, sharing, or mixing.' My old hippy soul would feel very uncomfortable if I were in his shoes. Having to be around all those massive egos boasting about their superiority. It must be exhausting trying to pretend you're the best and above everyone else all the time. What's best, anyhow? The best one can be? Fine, but better than anyone else?" Jonas laughed to himself. "You know what I think? I think VIP means *very idiotic people*!"

Vera laughed. "You must be the exception then. You were born into wealth, and yet you're such a nice person, a brilliant teacher, and always ready to help."

Jonas smiled bashfully. "Why, thank you. So glad you told me all that. I guess my parents never allowed me to lead a sheltered life . . . They didn't keep secrets from me, either, so I actually have no illusions about the power or glamour wealth seems to give. However, this student of mine, the young piano player, had fought his way into law school. A self-made young man who came from a family in which art was not valued. A *Great Gatsby* kind of character, you know? And this Dora was certainly as attractive to him as Daisy was heartless to her Gatsby."

"Heartless . . ." said Vera, pausing before adding, "she certainly no longer seemed to remember this student of yours, if her behavior at the fountain is anything to go by. She was trying to seduce Thomas and lure him to their house. Even I picked up on that. Where is this student of yours now?"

"He was suffering from severe depression. His family took him to stay with relatives in a small town in Minas Gerais, Brazil.

They were afraid he'd try to take his own life. He was devastated by everything that happened, so I asked around. Apparently, Alonso, his daughter, and his wife are the leaders of a cult that is somehow connected to musical traditions. He is a known collector of ancient instruments, you know. He also keeps ancient musical sheets and leads ceremonies so that people can play with his collection. His followers are all young and talented, mostly teenagers. During their time in his group, they all start to act differently, more superior. Most of them, however, have left their studies, not only here, at our university, but in other colleges as well. A friend of mine, a psychiatrist, told me she saw a student of his in a very deep crisis at the ER some months ago."

Vera thought about what Jonas had said, what he'd revealed, and it helped her make her decision. "Thank you for sharing all this, Jonas. I have Thomas's mobile number, and I'm going to call him and make sure everything is all right."

"Maybe you could invite him to perform at our spring bookfair when you talk to him. It would be great to have a talented musician entertain everyone."

Vera decided not to wait. She grabbed her phone and typed in the number. The call went to voicemail. She didn't leave a message. What could she tell him?

THOMAS'S JOURNAL

Conversations with the River

The practice of letting oneself dissolve into the flowing river waters—silent contemplation is a way to let one's mind travel to a dream-like state, becoming one with other living beings. Harmony, humbleness, wisdom, and peace. Sound healing.

A FISH, A FOX, AND A BIRD

Marlui dozed on the bus as she made her way back to the main road that led to the entrance of the preserved land.

"Are you tired, dear?"

She smiled at the senior citizen next to her.

"This is your final stop, is it not?" he asked her, pointing at the entrance gate.

"Thank you, sir!"

Going into the city was never easy. The long journey downtown exhausted her. Marlui climbed down the stairs of the bus and crossed the road toward the gate as fast as she could. Stepping through it, she sucked in an invigorating breath. The river greeted her, and she took off her sandals and made her way to the riverbank. She sat and sank her feet into the water, allowing it to run over her bare skin. She heard chatter and looked over her shoulder, smiling at her relatives crossing the bridge on their way to the village.

"Marlui, c'mon, let's go home!"

Hearing her native tongue spring from the children's mouths was like a soothing balm on her temples, and she felt herself reconnect to her soul. A feeling of deep comfort spread throughout her body. She dug her toes deeper into the riverbed. "I'll be there soon. Just a few minutes more," she called, waving to the children.

The first stars were beginning to poke through as the sun

dipped below the horizon. The grass moved softly in the cool breeze. Marlui hummed the melodies the musician had played. She'd never forget them, never forget him. Would they ever meet again?

Suddenly, Thomas's music seemed to echo across the riverbank as if he was there in the flesh. It sounded different, and her body shivered at the haunting beauty of his timeless melodies. Her body leaned back into the soft grass, her legs still in the water. Marlui felt herself becoming a fish, a fox, a bird girl. As she stared up at the moon, her eyes closed, and she slipped into a peaceful sleep. Her spirit left her body soaring into the night sky.

She found herself in an elegant room, hovering by his side while Thomas played an ancient instrument. People were sitting right in front of him, some with their eyes closed, others swaying as if in a deep trance. There was a musical sheet for him to follow, and the instrument seemed to have a life of its own. Marlui knew she couldn't use her normal senses when she traveled in spirit form. Sadness took over her. She wished she was there, not only in spirit but in her body, fully present. The musical instrument Thomas played captured her attention once more, like a powerful magnet she couldn't pull her gaze away from. It seemed ageless. If she touched it, would she be able to hear the echoes and melodies of its previous owners? She wondered then if Thomas was aware of its power. Could he sense the magic embedded in its wood? She pulled her gaze away. Who were the people around him? She looked closer, recognizing the father and daughter.

She instantly claimed the power of the jaguar guardian. Marlui's spirit dashed to Thomas's side, moving swiftly around the young musician to build a protective shield. As she did so, the teacher, the father, raised his glass as if to make a toast, but instead of drinking the wine, he moved toward Thomas and spilled the liquid around him, chanting some sort of magical verse. Marlui startled. Could he sense her presence? How? He was not a forest man—how could he see her, know she was there?

She knew he was trying to banish her, force her spirit to leave. Marlui wouldn't let him. She turned into her swallow self and perched at Thomas's left shoulder. She'd stay by his side, no matter what.

SECRETS IN THE GARDEN

"Please, Dora, stop kissing me. Let's just talk a bit!"

It was late afternoon, and try as he might, Thomas couldn't pull away from Dora or her commanding hands. She kept kissing his neck, his cheeks, and devouring his lips. He tried to kiss her back, he wanted to, but when he touched the long silky brown hair and realized his hands were tangled in a wig, a deep fear overwhelmed him. She wasn't who she seemed. In fact, he didn't really know who she was. He pulled away from her, watching her pout. He gulped and straightened his shirt before looking her directly in the eye. "What do you want from me, Dora?"

"What do you think I want? Look around, Thomas! We're sitting on a bench outside my house. We can't do anything. Why are you so afraid? Can't you just relax and enjoy this?"

"Relax? I don't think you're very relaxed, Dora. Why on earth are you wearing that wig again? I thought you were so comfortable here, so relaxed, you could at least be your own blonde self." Thomas rose from the bench. "I don't know what's going on here. You invited me to take a walk after lunch, to see the property. Then you beg me to sit here on your favorite bench. I'd barely touched the wood when you pounced on me, kissing me like you'd never get to kiss anyone ever again. There was no warning, not that I'm complaining, but I'm nobody's toy, Dora, and I won't be manipulated."

Dora stood and sidled up beside him. She laughed as she looked deep into his eyes. "I'm sorry, Thomas. I couldn't stop myself. There's something about you, something that draws me in, that's all, I promise. How about we take some pictures? Would you let me post them on my social media?"

"So, now, you're Dora, the influencer. Aren't you afraid of developing a split personality disorder?" Thomas teased, feeling a little more relaxed, and flattered that Dora found him irresistible. It was a new feeling.

"No, I'm not afraid. You see, both Doras, the blonde and the brunette, are very attracted to you, Thomas. There's nothing creepy about that, is there?"

"I didn't use the word creepy . . ." said Thomas as they left the bench and strolled under the tall, green trees. "But I must say, I'm not feeling very comfortable around you or your family. I have been meaning to leave since breakfast, to get back to my own home."

"You can leave whenever you want to," said Dora, looking as if she was going to cry. "What's bothering you? We've tried to make you comfortable . . ."

Thomas braced himself for what he was about to say. He didn't want to hurt her feelings or appear ungrateful. "It feels like I was lured here, mesmerized or something. I seem to have lost control of my situation. I had things to do at home, and here I am, just doing whatever you want me to do. What's next? What's in it for your father? He said he would show me the lute, but now I'm wondering, *why me*?"

Dora stopped walking, as if pondering what Thomas had just revealed. "I'll tell you about my father, then. Maybe that will help. As you can tell, we come from old money. For the past number of generations, my family has led secluded lives, you know those of the wealthy, trying to avoid being exploited or deceived, ensuring they weren't conned out of money. Besides having to endure the isolation growing up, my father was taught never to expose himself. You see, my grandparents were among the wealthiest of families in Latin America, and that meant the press would do their best to destroy any of us that tried to develop their own talents or do what normal people do, like you do, for instance."

"I'm not sure I understand, Dora, but at least we are having a normal conversation, and I'm glad you trust me enough to share your family secrets."

They strolled toward the swimming pool, and Dora sat in one of the summer armchairs. She motioned for Thomas to sit on the one next to her. The blue shimmering water seemed to calm him as he listened to her continue to explain.

"Dad was born with perfect pitch. My grandfather realized he had a very gifted son when he noticed Dad could whistle in total perfection any melody after only hearing it once. At school, his teachers noticed it too, and they suggested to my grandparents that Dad should embrace his talent and study music." Dora brushed her hair away from her face. "The thing was . . . my grandfather was really strict and always suspicious of people who he thought were trying to take away his money or possessions. He'd never had to deal with a gift like Dad's musical one. And he couldn't understand that it should be shared."

"What happened?" Thomas noticed the tears filling Dora's eyes and reached over to take her hand.

"He forbade my father from whistling in the school. He thought the whistling would attract more attention. You have to understand, grandfather had spent his life trying to prevent his family from being kidnapped. He had bodyguards, black sedans, maximum security, and so on. He was totally obsessed. He did what he thought was right and hired the best teacher money could buy. Of course, my dad's music tutor was a complete snob and totally neurotic. He came to the house every day and made my father listen to classical music for hours on end. He forced him to whistle or hum the melodies over and over. He couldn't believe a small child could be so musically sensitive. He traumatized my father, and when he finally introduced Dad to musical instruments, the piano being the first, Dad couldn't produce the notes to the perfection his tutor wanted. He had to practice, of course. But the tutor was impatient and harsh. He wouldn't allow Dad to play in the garden, watch TV, or just have some free time for himself like other kids his age. In the end, Dad developed a learning block, and he couldn't whistle anymore. He went through a period of depression, and as he grew up, he convinced my grandfather that he would rather study law. His decision pleased the whole family because studying law seemed a lot more reasonable than being a musician."

"How did he find out about me? The way I relate to music has nothing to do with your father's tragic story."

"Well, my mother has always been passionate about myths, rites, and magic, so when they met, she felt deeply sorry for the suffering Dad went through as a little child. She decided she would connect him to music again and made him go through an ancient rite. Dad loved it and developed an obsession for her obsession. They traveled all over the world, buying old instruments and listening to the most skilled musicians. They also took time out to learn magic from the most powerful mages money can buy. My parents believe money can buy everything, but when it comes to real talent and powerful magic, money can't buy it. They have tried to lure indigenous people to the house so they could perform musical rituals for our group, but they refused, making all types of excuses."

"Such as?" Thomas wasn't sure where this conversation was going.

"Bad spirits, bad intentions, and things like that. So, Dad doesn't really like them. Fact is, his dream has always been to find naturally gifted young people and invite them over to play his beloved instruments, using the ancient musical sheets he's managed to collect over the years. Please, try to understand him and where he's coming from, Thomas. Don't be so judgmental."

"You haven't told me how he found me yet."

"I did. I read an interview you gave on TV some time ago. I've been following you on social media. I've even seen you play several times before. I knew you liked playing in the square near the university. Anyway, when Dad heard you, he realized you must have been as gifted as he was as a child. So, I guess he wants to see you play, hear what he could have been if my grandfather hadn't taken his gift away."

"Okay then, I will stay." Thomas settled back in the chair. "Besides, I really want to play an authentic medieval lute."

Dora launched toward him before he could react, landing on his lap and smacking her lips against his. Her hands curled in his hair, at the nape of his neck. She licked his bottom lip, encouraging him to open up to her. Thomas couldn't resist any longer. He wrapped his hands around her waist, pulled her closer, and kissed her back.

DANCING TO THE MUSIC

Gabriella loved hearing Manuel and André laughing around the house. So playful, her two little sources of inspiration. She left her studio and went to the kitchen to fix them a snack, watermelon juice and carrot cake.

As she set down the cake slices and poured the watermelon juice into two glasses, she heard a familiar melody. She turned to see the boys entering the kitchen. "What song is that? I'm sure I've heard it before, but just can't recall where or when . . . It's very beautiful."

They both laughed before singing the tune together in perfect harmony. She remembered instantly. It was one of Thomas's songs. One he'd played that afternoon by the fountain.

"What a beautiful song, boys." Jonas's cheerful voice echoed from the hallway.

Gabriella smiled as she heard his footsteps approaching. She loved their evening routine, chatting in the kitchen with Jonas while she prepared dinner. Then they would both tuck the boys into bed before she had her shower. The remainder of the evening was spent reading and enjoying each other's company.

"Do you think our boys are musically gifted?" Jonas asked, taking a carton of orange juice out of the fridge.

Gabriella passed him an empty glass. She hated when he drank straight from the carton. "Perhaps. They were so impressed with Thomas. I can't stop thinking about how they dreamt about him before they'd even met. I've also been thinking about how they were the ones who insisted we go to the square, that they were supposed to meet a new friend there . . ."

Jonas rested his arms on the countertop. "Oh, dear . . . are you sure you're not adding more meaning to this than is necessary? I mean, they're just kids being kids, but I do think they might have a musical gift. The other day, I was reading about people who have a perfect pitch. Have you heard about it?"

Gabriella smiled as she washed the fresh lettuce for the salad. She loved her creative madness, but she also enjoyed Jonas's pragmatic ways. His world was the world of law, human rights, and, yes, the quest for justice. As she chose the most colorful tomatoes to add to the green dish, she turned to him. "Actually, yes, I did hear about it. The other day, I was researching savant kids. Young minds in the autistic spectrum, socially awkward yet so gifted in mathematics and music . . ."

Jonas reached for the paper towel to clean the drops of juice that had landed on the counter. Gabriella smiled; she appreciated his cleanliness and meticulous gestures.

Jonas smiled back. "Our boys are very social, so I guess they wouldn't fit into that description. But I am curious now that you've mentioned it."

Gabriella laughed, wiped her hands on her apron, and ran to her studio. She returned with her laptop, opening it up on the dining room table. The definition she'd found was still on the screen. She read it out loud. "The term *absolute pitch recognition* is the ability to recognize musical notes immediately, as well as the ability to produce (singing or whistling) any pitch on immediate demand."

"Can the ability be acquired?" asked Jonas, setting the table.

"Yes, I mean, musical sensibility can actually be enhanced by musical education."

"Perhaps we should buy our boys some musical toys," said Jonas.

"Ha, that rhymes. I like the idea though.

"Please say we're having French fries tonight?" groaned André, bursting into the dining room.

"I can fix some, if you'd like," said Jonas.

"Yeah," André said, and Manuel chimed in at the same time.

As the boys sat at the table, still humming Thomas's song, Jonas turned to them. "Have you memorized this song?"

"Memorized?" asked André. "Not really."

"How come you seem to know it so well? It's great that you do. You could have perfect musical memory recall or even perfect pitch.

"Perfect pitch?" asked Manuel. "What's that?"

Jonas smiled as he thought of how to explain it in terms the boys could understand. "Well, it's the ability to listen to a melody once and be able to memorize it and immediately sing or whistle it."

"Wow! Cool!" both of them said. Then André added, "But that's not what's happening."

"Oh. Who taught you the song?" asked Gabriella, fully focused on the conversation.

"The dancing creatures."

Gabriella looked confused. "What dancing creatures?"

André looked disappointed. "Can't you see them, Mom? They are so much fun!"

CAPTURA

"For your eyes only!"

Dr. Alonso triumphantly handed the lute to Thomas with a large smile on his face.

As Thomas held the lute, he positioned himself in the chair and greeted the select audience. His mind recalled the strange conversation about the lute they had over dinner.

"I bought this lute from a very exclusive collector in France. I knew I would eventually find a real-life Troubadour to play it, Thomas. The collector told me this instrument may have been played by the legendary Guiraut Riquier. I'm not sure if that's true, and I think this lute was probably made later, but I did find an anonymous medieval manuscript with it. Would you like to play sheet music? It's a song meant to express happiness and peace. The composition is derived from a Latin sequence. The main chords are composed according to the principles of cosmic harmony."

Thomas pulled himself back to the present and greeted his audience with a smile. "Good evening, everyone. I hope you enjoy this piece." He opened the sheet music, expecting a title such as "Joy and Peace," but it simply read, *Captura.* He also expected to find lyrics, but the sheets contained only notes. He read them quickly, afraid he'd make a fool of himself. He regretted not asking Dr. Alonso for a chance to study the manuscript carefully before the recital.

As he read the music, another of Dr. Alonso's strange

statements came to mind. He'd said, "Beauty is only for the few. Vulgar people cannot appreciate it. History has witnessed the relentless destruction of beauty over and over. War, greed, ignorance, intolerance—I don't believe in sharing. Art should belong exclusively to those who are truly capable of fully appreciating it. I am a unique keeper of beauty and so are my disciples."

Thomas took a deep breath and bowed his head to Dr. Alonso. A deep sense of gratitude overtook his heart. He knew he was about to experience something extraordinary.

Dr. Alonso smiled back. He looked comfortable in his seat as he stared at Thomas. Thomas began to play. As his fingers moved swiftly over the strings, he closed his eyes. The notes appeared in his mind, and he followed them. He knew he didn't need to read the sheet music. A smile spread across his face, and the feeling of joy he always felt when in the company of his secret sound creatures enlarged his soul. Ancient landscapes, fields, castles, public squares—he heard his music echoing across time and place. He lost himself in the music.

Pain—sudden and piercing pain pulled him from his musical reverie. The tips of his fingers were covered in blood, but he had no command over them. He couldn't stop playing the instrument. He looked around at the audience, eyes begging for help, but no one seemed to notice the drops of blood slowly and steadily staining his pants.

He wanted to break the trance, to disobey the lute's relentless command, but he couldn't. Tears filled his eyes, spilling over his cheeks. Another layer of pain seemed to grip him. His reflection in the window revealed bulging eyes, his long hair now gray. Deep lines were appearing around his mouth. *A death trap. I have to stop playing*, he thought. But he couldn't—his fingers kept strumming, the instrument producing music, as Thomas struggled to break its hold.

A cry pierced his ears. Not a human one, but a bird scream. A snarl. A jaguar. Where was this coming from? Something was warning him of the imminent danger, the fatality it would produce. He knew he had to stop, to leave immediately. With all the force he could muster, he pulled his fingers away from the strings. Pain shot through his body, but he kept going. He interrupted the recital, and with bloodshot eyes and a dry mouth, he rose and placed the lute on the chair. He bolted out of the room; applause and shouts of bravo following him. He could hear them even as the door closed behind him. No one followed. No one came to see him or ask for an encore. He'd escaped—for now.

FORBIDDEN TRAVELS

"Take your feet out of the river." Popygua pulled Marlui back onto the riverbank. He held his beloved grandchild tenderly and hummed a healing melody. He looked up at the stars, tears pooling in his eyes. Was he too late? He could sense her pain. It was intertwined with someone else's suffering. Could it be the soul of the guitar player he had seen in his vision?

As Marlui recovered, she seemed so ashamed of herself. "I'm so sorry, Grandpa. I knew I shouldn't have let my spirit travel so far away. But I just had to help him, you see. And the river allowed me to go to him."

"You young people are so reckless. If you want to protect this young fellow, you must bring him to me. You can't take it upon yourself. He must want your help. Otherwise, you won't be able to share your energy with him properly. This is why we, and the ancestors, have always forbidden young people from spirit traveling."

Marlui stood, looked at the moon, heaved a deep sigh. "I'm not even sure he remembers my name. To him, I'm probably just some unusual girl who watched him play. I don't think he knows much about us, Grandpa, or our culture and ways."

Popygua guided Marlui slowly back to the road that led to their house. "Are you sure he deserves your attention . . . your affection?"

Marlui laughed. She was starting to feel like her old self again. "It's not only about affection, Grandpa. The world outside can be so violent, shallow, and greedy, but I saw his soul, and it's all about beauty and goodness. This musician is also a healer, even if he is not aware of it. He shouldn't be left to die or have his gift taken away from him. I sense this is what those people are trying to do. I need your help, Grandpa . . . Please, help me."

"Young souls . . ." Popygua shook his head. "You want to do what you want to do, no matter the consequences . . . Let's drink some tea, your grandma will fix you a good meal, and then you can have a good night's sleep. We'll talk about the boy then."

THE GATHERING

Vera looked around the square. It was later afternoon, downtown, and the tall trees threw thin shadows over the two elderly chess players that had caught her attention. The aroma of sweet cotton reminded her of her childhood, and out of impulse, she found herself purchasing some popcorn and sitting on the nearest bench. A strong sense of peace enveloped the square, and Vera sat, savoring the taste of salt, as girlish memories sprung to life.

"Vera! Is that you?"

Vera looked up to see Gabriella taking the seat beside her. "Oh, hello there."

"It's so quiet, and while I do love the peace, I must admit, I miss the music now," Gabriella said.

Hearing their mother's words, André and Manuel left their toys aside and started whistling.

"That's Thomas's song!" Vera said. "Stunning! They can whistle it perfectly. Your boys are truly gifted."

Gabriella smiled proudly. "Thank you. They've never done that before. I mean, they usually hum or sing children's lullabies. I never in my wildest dreams imagined them being able to memorize such a complex melody."

"Mom!" Manuel said, holding his mother's gaze. "I told you before! We can hear the dancing creatures. That's why we can sing like them."

Vera shook her head in awe. Was it just a childish game, or could these kids actually see invisible creatures? She sighed deeply. A wave of sadness pinched her heart as she suddenly missed her own mother. Her mother tried to explain the invisible friends she saw and heard to people, whilst Vera, even as a small child, would contradict her. She had never shared her mother's love for fairy tales, and now these two boys were trying to show her something that her mother had once tried to tell her. Vera suddenly wished she'd allowed her mother to share more of her knowledge, no matter how peculiar it may have sounded to a young, restless girl like her. Her mom was probably lonely, caught between Dad and her impatience . . . two skeptical minds. Vera remained silent until another voice broke the reverie.

"May I ask what color your creatures are?" Marlui then turned and greeted Vera and Gabriella.

"Green, of course." André giggled. "They're like dancing leaves and all different shapes. Can't you see them?"

"Yes, I can!" said Marlui as she stooped low to hug André.

"I wish I could join you, Marlui." Vera sighed. "I'd love to tell the kids my imagination still allows me to see invisible beings, but it's real life that matters to me. And if I'm honest, I came here today in the hopes of meeting you both again, and I'm so glad I have the chance to talk to you now. I have been really upset about this whole thing . . ."

Gabriella moved closer to Vera. "What do you mean? What the whole thing?"

"I wish I had good news to share. I wish I could tell you that Thomas will be back and will play here again, but I feel like something is wrong. I'm so worried about him, I even made up a lame excuse to call him."

"I tried calling him too!" Gabriella said.

"I thought of inviting him to play at the university's spring festival, maybe not the best excuse, but it was all I could think of at the time."

"That's an excellent excuse," said Marlui. "And you really should invite him."Marlui reached across and helped herself to some of Vera's popcorn. She watched the branches on the trees sway as she pondered how to tell her new friends what she really thought was happening with Thomas. Determined to get it out, she cleared her throat. "I know you're both city people, but I really do have to share something with you. It might seem a little extraordinary, but please listen with an open mind. As I got home yesterday evening, the river spirits called me. I sat by the riverbank and stared at the waters. Then I let my spirit travel and find Thomas. I wanted to be close to him. I sensed he could be in danger." Marlui paused to gauge their reaction before continuing, "Forgive me if I sound a bit crazy, but this is how we sense things among my people. Anyway, I had a vision, and it was not a good one . . . I'm convinced Thomas is in trouble."

Vera opened her bag and took out several sheets of paper, clippings with pictures and newspaper articles. "Well, dear friends, I too am sure Thomas is in trouble. Although I didn't have visions like you, Marlui. Don't get me wrong, my mother also believed in the supernatural . . ."

Marlui smiled. "We don't believe in the supernatural. I mean, visions are natural among our traditions . . ."

Vera smiled back before continuing, "Let's say unnatural things might be happening to Thomas. Look at these clippings I've found. Apparently, my colleague Dr. Alonso has already been sued for recruiting young people to very strange parties. The reason why these young people's parents were upset is because all these poor kids seemed to be somehow psychologically damaged after taking part in their ceremonies. Some even had to be committed to clinics, although there was no substance ingestion involved. There's something very off about the whole thing."

Gabriella stood from the bench, her finger tapping her chin. "Do you have Dr. Alonso's address or phone number? I mean, I am sure Jonas could get it, but he is teaching at the moment."

"I do," said Vera, "but apparently his house is kept under high security, with guards and everything. If you're thinking we should go there and try to rescue Thomas from whatever danger he might be facing, it won't be easy. Besides, he's a lawyer. We could actually give him grounds to sue us for trespassing."

Marlui wrapped her arms around herself as a chilling breeze surrounded her. The three of them remained silent as the two boys hummed the mesmerizing song they'd heard Thomas play just a day before.

Vera spoke first. "How about we keep in touch? Let's exchange mobile numbers. Who knows, one of us might come up with a good idea."

"I'll talk to Jonas tonight. He will certainly help us. He has been complaining about this Dr. Alonso person for a while now," said Gabriella.

Vera stood up and proceeded to kiss her new friends goodbye. Before she left the square, she paused. "The thing is, Jonas and I have been trying to figure this all out. We had a meeting at the school coffee shop, and you are right, Gabriella, your husband does seem to mistrust the man as well."

"So do I," Gabriella and Marlui both said at the same time.

RIGHT NOW

"Marlui, let's take a walk in the woods," said Popygua.

It was dusk, and as they moved slowly toward a clearing, the full moon lit the way. They were used to night walks in the forest, and Popygua sang the secret songs to appease the night spirits. Marlui had not yet been taught the primordial language of timeless melodies, but she did her best to try and sing along. She knew the forest spirits must give their permission to allow humans to cross the night tracks in safety.

The sacred tree right in the middle of the clearing was tall and strong, the large roots spreading themselves over the soil. Popygua wrapped his arms around the wide tree trunk and held it for a few moments before taking a seat on one of the largest outspread roots. He waited for Marlui to copy his actions. Marlui placed a hand on the tree trunk, feeling a deep sense of gratitude fill her, being grateful for the tree's presence and the forest that surrounded them. As Marlui stooped to sit next to her grandpa, he gestured for her to look at the sky before opening his arms, as if to gather the moonlight's strength. Marlui copied him, and for the next half an hour, they both sat in silence.

Marlui caressed the large roots and felt deep peace and comfort. Her head rested against the trunk, and her eyelids grew heavy. She was about to close them when Popygua started talking to her.

"You should not feel guilty for his loss, my child . . ."

Tears flooded Marlui's eyes. She knew Popygua was referring to the loss of her best friend, Kaue. She tried to avoid the memory, the moment he smiled at her and jumped off the waterfall. They swam together in the river every day, they spent every afternoon together, they confided in each other, and they knew their friendship was true and loving. But somehow, Kaue's life was taken from him; he slipped and fell, death instantly taking him from her. "It was my fault. I called his name; that's why he turned and lost his balance . . ."

Popygua cupped her face and waited patiently as she released the deep pain from within, sobbing openly as tears streamed down her cheeks.

"Kaue was our best swimmer, my child. How many times had you called him before and nothing happened? His days were over, that's all. It was his time to move on to another land . . . When we go through our daily lives, we think we are living in one single world. But this is not true. We walk through many different lands day and night without really knowing. Kaue is just on the other side of the river, the third bank, the dwelling of all our ancestors, or maybe he chose to become a beautiful star in the invisible constellation of the afterlife. You cannot see him now, but I am sure he can see you. I know he still loves you, and he always will."

"I will never forget him. I will never love anyone like I loved him . . ." Marlui wiped away the remaining tears with her shirt.

Popygua laughed and caressed her hand. "Of course not. Kaue is Kaue, and you are you. When you love again, it will be different, and that's right, but it also will be the same, because the true nature of love never changes." He looked up at Marlui, his expression serious. "Now, you can tell me the truth. Are you afraid this young musician's life is at stake? You see, my child, once we see someone departing right in front of our eyes as you have, we learn to sense the atmosphere that surrounds a soul when they are prone to leave this life. Is it what you felt?"

Marlui kept her thoughts to herself for a few seconds, trying to find the answer to her grandfather's question inside of her. Finally, she answered, "When Kaue left this world, I felt like following him. A death wish. You remember how I lost all interest in life . . . But slowly, and with your help, and the help of all our relatives, I realized my time had not come, and I could enjoy being alive again."

Popygua hugged her, looked up at the tree, and said an ancient prayer.

Marlui continued, "Anyway, I realized I had died in some way. I was no longer the same reckless girl. I was a new me, someone who knew the pain of loss, someone who came through it."

Popygua put a blanket over his grandchild's shoulders and asked her to go on.

"I am not sure the young musician is about to die in the flesh, at least not now. But I had this painful feeling that his soul was about to leave this life somehow. You always taught me that a sick spirit has to be healed; otherwise, the body will be ill as well. I felt as if his spirit and body were about to be torn apart. You must help him. I feel so privileged to be your grandchild, and I wish all young people could rely on your wisdom and knowing."

Popygua was silent for a few moments before he took a deep breath. "When you first saw and heard him, downtown, my spirit was summoned by his music. I can recall his sounds. It was the echo of Earth's voice, the singing of birds, waterfalls, very beautiful indeed."

"Yes, it is true. I wish we could bring him here. To be with us for a while."

"A musician and a healer share the same path; they spend their lives traveling, speaking beyond words, and rescuing ancient memories of wisdom and hope from people's hearts . . . Yes, Marlui, I agree with you. We should try and bring him here. If his soul needs help, I will be able to sense it better if he is among us."

"Oh, thank you so much, Grandpa. When could we do that?"

"The past does not belong to us, the future is yet to come, all we have is right now, and right now it should be."

THOMAS'S JOURNAL

"A musician and a healer share the same path; they spend their lives traveling, speaking beyond words, and rescuing ancient memories of wisdom and hope from people's hearts .. ."

MANUSCRIPTS

As much as Thomas had insisted that he wanted to study the musical sheet before his presentation that evening, he just could not get ahold of it. Thomas had thought he escaped from his hosts. He wanted to be alone in the guest room to study the musical sheet before his presentation.

"Give me some space today, Dora, please," he said after they'd eaten lunch together. "I feel so tired. I need to get some rest."

He entered the bedroom and was about to lie on the bed when someone knocked. Thomas expected it would be Dr. Alonso with the musical sheet he'd requested, but it turned out to be the maid.

"Dr. Alonso said you should read this." She handed him an old book on troubadours and walked away.

Thomas sat on the armchair in his room with the book perched on his knees. His need for a nap was forgotten as he opened the cover. As he prepared to read, a strange and deep longing for trees came over him. Thomas had always been fond of nature—but he wasn't a tree hugger, and truth be known, he'd always been more interested in listening to the birds than the trees or plants. He pulled the armchair closer to the window and took in the tall eucalyptus that swayed elegantly as if entranced by music of their own making. He shook his head, admiring the beautiful cover adorned with a medieval representation of a troubadour. He opened the book to a random page and read:

"The musical manuscripts that belonged to the troubadours are full of secrets. They date from the XIII century, mostly, but their origins are very hard to define. Nobody really knows how the collected songs were placed into these manuscripts. Who selected them? Who were the authors? Even if the songs of Guiraut Riquier (1254-1292), one of the last troubadours, were carefully dated and presented in a manuscript by the artist himself, several details will never be found. Some songs are attributed to certain composers. Is this information trustworthy?

What about the melodies? It is easy to find several variations of the same melodies from one manuscript to another. Who were the composers of these songs?

Maybe one should consider the possibility of having several different lyricists and composers in the manuscripts, multiple voices belonging not only to anonymous poets but to the singers as well?

Thomas closed the book and thought for a second about the origin of his own music. He'd never told anyone about the singing sound creatures that surrounded him. As a little boy, people told him they were just a figment of his imagination, and he realized as he got older that mentioning his relationship with them would lead to scorn or accusations of a mental disorder.

It was a lonely existence, and in the solitude of his room, he wondered if his secret had been a heavy burden to bear. How could he feel alone while surrounded by such beautiful creatures? He wondered about authorship and what it meant. He usually heard the melodies and then tried to convey the songs. It took a lot of effort, research, practice, and study to become a musician good enough to translate all the joy these musical creatures brought into his life. He had to find the right tone, the best way to perform the songs, and the proper atmosphere required to share them with people.

Now, however, he was truly alone. A haunting emptiness had settled within him, and he missed the company of his musical beings. He couldn't understand why they'd left him or why he felt so depleted.

Throughout his life, he'd experienced several states of exhaustion. Being physically tired after playing for hours on end, sleepless nights, and walking miles without regard, entranced by the musical beings' songs, realizing late at night that he must turn around before he gets lost.

In this strange house, he'd slept soundly. He'd eaten very well. He hadn't had any physical exertion, but still, he felt weak. He was overwhelmed by an eerie feeling of having been deprived of some inner, sacred stamina he'd always taken for granted.

He couldn't concentrate on the book, he couldn't sleep, and he didn't feel hungry either. He wanted to leave the house, but some strange unbearable desire was forcing him to stay. Was it the lute or perhaps Dora's allure that was holding him hostage? Was he falling in love with her? Thomas shook his head. No. There was no deep affection between them. They belonged to two very different worlds, and he felt no empathy toward her so-called troubles. A lingering feeling of distrust remained no matter what she said. To him, it felt as if she was complaining about a fake tragedy and problems that didn't seem like much of a burden to bear.

Her father, on the other hand, was an exceptional man. He wore the cloak of someone trying to live up to an old dream. All he wanted was to listen to a true troubadour playing an authentic lute with music from a rare manuscript. As he thought it, a sense of dread welled inside of him. What if it was all an act? What if Dr. Alonso were someone much more dangerous and sinister than his demeanor seemed to indicate? What if he was some kind of sorcerer? This unsettled him more than ever. What if he was being kept in the house of some malignant lord?

A whistle penetrated his thoughts. It sounded of similar quality to his musical creature's voices. He rose from the chair and whistled back, joy surging through him once more as he realized the music was still with him. He could hear beyond his own ears, and he could sing beyond the sounds.

Thomas rushed to the window. He was sure the whistle came from outside. He peered through the glass. Then he became startled. A man with white hair and huge dark eyes was staring up at him. A smile graced his face before he started singing. It was a language Thomas had never heard before, and yet he sensed that the man's voice held the tones of the trees, the rivers, and the skies. Who was he? Was he a delusion, or was he real?

THE WEB

"Hello, Marlui! Glad to find you here!" Vera said.

Marlui took the laptop and sat on the roots of the large mango tree. In the village, everybody knew that this was the best place for the internet signal. The lamp by the tree provided light. Marlui smiled back as she saw Vera's face appearing. "Hello, Vera. You sound surprised. Did you not think we'd have the internet here?"

"Well, I must say, I thought you forest people were against technology." Vera blushed, embarrassed by her lack of knowledge.

"Of course not. The internet exchange has really helped us fight for our rights and the protection of the environment."

Vera moved closer to the laptop which sat on the desk of her home office. "So, you actually accept that modern life has its advantages, right?"

Marlui peeled a banana and replied calmly, "Oh, yes, we have always valued communication, no matter how. But people like you, born and raised in the city, also like our ways, don't you?

"How so?" Vera said, her tone a little defiant.

"Hello, girls!" Gabriella joined the conversation. She'd placed her laptop on the kitchen table. Jonas and the boys were watching television. Jonas had promised to do the nightly routine with the boys. It meant that Gabriella had the whole evening to chat online with Vera and Marlui. "What were you talking about? Sorry, I came in a bit late."

"I was asking Vera if she had realized how much you, city people, have learned from us, forest dwellers, the originating nations," said Marlui.

"Go on, I am curious now," Gabriella said, reaching for the glass of juice beside her.

Marlui peeled her second banana and gave it to the little monkey perched on her shoulder. "For starters, did you take a shower today?"

"What a weird question," said Vera. "Of course, I did. During summer, I take two or even three showers a day."

"Well, when European people arrived in Brazil, they hated bathing. They were constantly afraid of getting colds and dying. So, slowly, they realized that the river was a good friend, and keeping one's body really clean would be much better for their health. Grandpa says that God gave the forests, the healing herbs, the rivers, and the animals to all of humanity. But only we forest keepers knew how to love and protect them. We have lived wisely and peacefully for hundreds of years, and our interaction with nature, which seemed so primitive to the first Europeans, is actually very ecological and up to date. I have heard people refer to us as these 'primitive third world people.' We don't believe in a world divided by three. Everyone should share their knowledge. In the city, people only value what's new . . . We are not new, you see? We have lived in the forest for centuries, and we certainly know a lot about preservation."

"Yes, you do have a point there, don't you, Marlui?" Vera said.

"Let me go on . . ." Marlui said in a more stern, harsh manner. "Don't you love eating bananas, like me? Don't you love taking your time contemplating nature or sunbathing on a beach or by the river? These are all habits of ours. Can't you see that? Have you ever thought about all the native fruit and healing herbs that are now part of your daily life? Our culture is rich and healthy, but it has been recorded orally, from mouth to ear, and all you seem to value is the printed word. This is one of the reasons why you cannot identify or define our knowledge as such."

Vera smiled and said, "Dear Marlui, you are very good at advocating for your people. Is this why you want to become a lawyer? To fight for your rights? You are welcome into my class, you know. You do have a sound cause; I must give you that. You must not resent me. You are the first Guarani young woman I have ever talked to. We live in a strange scenario, here in São Paulo. Your forest is just two hours away from my flat. Yet it never occurred to me to go and visit, to talk to you people. I guess I must make up for the time lost.

Marlui laughed out loud. She enjoyed Vera's acceptance of her arguments. A baby monkey and his mother came down the trees. Marlui allowed the baby to perch on her shoulder.

Gabriella quickly took notes in her journal. Ideas were coming to her as she listened intently to their conversation. When her boys came close to kiss her goodnight, they saw Vera and Marlui with her cute baby monkey.

"Wow! Hello, Marlui!" They greeted her.

"Hi, boys! You should come and visit us sometime soon," Marlui said, waving at them both.

"We certainly will," said Jonas, coming close to the laptop screen to greet her and Vera before telling the boys it was time for bed. "Don't go anywhere, though. I have some news to share with you."

It took him a record five minutes to get the boys settled before he appeared in front of the screen. "I'll make this short. We all witnessed the exact moment Thomas was recruited by Dr. Alonso, right? But can anyone explain to me why he was so easily recruited?"

Gabriella was the first to answer. "I heard Dr. Alonso mention a medieval lute when he was suggesting Thomas should visit. He said he could play it, this rare instrument that he kept in his home. He acted like he was some sort of collector of valuable musical instruments. Perhaps that's why Thomas agreed. Dr. Alonso appealed to the musician in him."

Jonas remained silent for a few moments. "Yes, you're probably right. My guess is that he uses his private collection as bait, as well as his beautiful daughter, Dora."

The full moon attracted Marlui's attention. She felt like leaving the call and going into the forest meadow to pray for Thomas, but she forced herself to stay a bit longer. She also wanted information about this whole scenario. As night spread its dark mantle over the trees, danger seemed to be hovering, and she didn't want to rely solely on her intuition, no matter how strong it could be. She tapped a finger against her chin. "Jonas, do you think Thomas might be putting his mental health at stake? I mean, I would hate to see Thomas as depressed as that other student of yours, Rafael. You told me some time ago that he had to leave college to be with his family in Minas Gerais . . ."

"Unfortunately, yes. I have a feeling this gifted friend of yours could very well be Dr. Alonso's latest prey. The problem is, I'm not sure what we can do about it?"

Vera excused herself for a moment before holding up an old book to the screen. It was engraved with golden letters that said, *The Emerald Table*. "This book belonged to my late, beloved mother. It is a very rare edition. I guess we could call it our bait . . . Do you think Dr. Alonso would want to buy it?"

Gabriella smiled. "Guys, this is even more exciting than any detective story I could dream up . . . What about we all barge into one of his parties using the book as an excuse?"

"It's too late now," Jonas said. "It's already 10:30 p.m., and if there is a party going on, it'll have started already. I really hope Thomas can survive whatever Alonso has planned for him. I definitely would like to hear him play again."

Marlui had remained quiet, trying to decide whether she should share her secret. Were these people really her friends? She decided it was better to take that chance, to trust them. "Grandpa has said exactly the same thing, Jonas. He definitely wants to listen to Thomas's music!"

"Am I missing something here? What are you trying to tell us, Marlui? I don't get it, Marlui! Sometimes you sound so down-to-earth. Next moment you talk about your grandpa having supernatural powers. What are you trying to tell us?" Vera said.

"I am not sure you would understand. All I can say is that Popygua, my grandpa, has his own ways. Today, right after lunch, he invited me to go to the heart of the woods. We sat at the meadow for a couple of hours, listening to the trees and birds. Of course, I told him about Thomas. Then, he asked me to leave him alone. He hasn't come back home. He is still there, at our sacred meadow. This is all I am allowed to tell you . . . I must join him now!"

WHITE SILK

A knock on the door. Thomas turned from the window and opened it to reveal the maid.

"May I come in?" she asked.

Thomas quickly turned toward the window to check if the old man was still there, smiling at him. To his relief, he was. He swayed his body in a strange sort of dance, waving, and Thomas felt his piercing eyes looking right through him.

"Who's that?" Thomas asked the maid, pointing to the man. "He's so striking. Does he live in the forest? You have a beautiful forest outside."

The maid, who had a package in her hands, walked to the window and looked out. "I'm so sorry, sir. There is no one outside . . . What are you talking about?"

Thomas thought about telling her that yes, there was an old man standing, waving, and smiling at him by the eucalyptus tree, just beyond the garden, but then he realized it would be pointless—she couldn't see him. "Oh, silly me," he said, "I must have been mistaken."

She handed him the package and nodded. "The tall trees by the yard. Sometimes they cast long shadows."

Thomas frowned. Obviously, this man was similar to his unheard sounds, and he wouldn't be able to share it with anyone. *I could be going insane*, he thought. His hands quivered.

"Are you cold?" the maid asked, staring at his shaking hands.

"It certainly gets chilly here, in the evening. Dr. Alonso has asked me to bring you this."

Thomas thanked her and waited until she left the room to open the box. He removed the black lid to reveal a white silk cloak. *Strange*, he thought. He lifted it from the box and then saw the golden collar. *Maybe there's a costume party tonight. These people are nuts. I have to get out of here.*

He tucked the cloak back into the box before picking up his guitar and walking toward the landline phone to call a cab. Thomas regretted not having charged his mobile as soon as he arrived at Dora's. Another knock on the door interrupted him. Feeling deeply annoyed, Thomas mumbled to himself as he turned toward the door. He planned to tell whoever it was that he was leaving. The door opened, and there she was—Dora.

Thomas just stared as he took her in—the long, white, silk, Greek-style tunic with a plunging neckline, showing off her cleavage, her short blonde hair, and her sumptuous lips which spread across her face in a tempting and teasing smile.

"Dinner is ready, Thomas. You'll need your cloak."

Mesmerized or somehow overwhelmed by the perfect classical beauty, Thomas quictly placed his mobile on the bedside table, opened the box, put on the strange, swaying, silk white cloak, and followed her through the long corridor that led to the dining room.

NIGHTMARISH LULLABY

Gabriella sat on her bed. Perhaps she'd be better off just going downstairs to write. There were so many doubts, unsettling thoughts, and deep fears preventing her from getting a good night's sleep. Writing always settled her, even if she couldn't think of gripping plots and scenes. The act of writing itself is what brought calmness. She glanced at Jonas sleeping soundly by her side. She slipped out of bed, careful not to wake him. Maybe she'd stop by the boys' room to make sure they were sleeping. She loved to look at them while they slept, so peaceful.

"Mom!"

Manuel opened the door so fast she didn't have time to kneel so he could hug her. "Look!" He pointed toward his brother.

Gabriela shivered. André was sitting on the carpet, eyes closed, little arms wrapped around his rocking body, humming a very unusual melody. It was no longer Thomas's song, but something else entirely. In fact, the sound was so unusual that she couldn't define it. Some sort of nightmarish lullaby.

Manuel gripped her hand tightly and whispered, "André got out of bed and sat like this, and he won't stop humming that ugly song. I have tried to wake him up. I am sure it is a nightmare, but he won't listen to me."

"Don't try to wake him!"

Gabriella let out a sigh of relief at the sound of Jonas's voice. He moved slowly and carefully lowered himself to the carpet. He gestured for Manuel and Gabriella to do the same. "It could be a type of sleepwalking. Whatever you do, don't touch him or try to wake him. We'll just sit here with him and wait to see what happens."

WELCOME TO THE ORPHICS

Thomas noticed that the lamps in the long, winding corridor had been replaced with old, large, bronze torches. The eerie, timeless atmosphere was enhanced by the illusion the flames were breathing in and out.

He turned slowly and saw the open windows. *This is why the fire is swaying. It's just the breeze coming in from outside. There's nothing to be frightened about. The house is safe*, he thought.

Dora also stopped and turned back, smiling at him. She gestured seductively, inviting him to follow her, but Thomas felt a sudden urge to look through the open window. Would he be able to see the old man again?

As he gazed at the starlit sky, he missed his sound creatures so deeply. A part of him seemed to be missing, torn away. He'd only experienced a pain similar once before. His soul ached as the memories of his parents' sudden loss filled his mind. The car accident at night. Thomas, still a ten-year-old boy, being rescued by the policemen. The long days in the hospital. Being told later that he had inherited the family house and that his parents had left him enough money to go through two lifetimes. Staying months at his parent's friend's house. His reluctance to go back home just to find it empty. Yet, when he was finally brave enough to go back home, he found the house was full of unexpected surprises— his secret sound creatures. They had remained in his bedroom waiting for his return. Once he reconnected with music, Thomas could play, sing, and most of all, listen to and rejoice in the beauty of life surrounding him.

"Thomas, look!"

Dora took his hand and led him into the dining room. Large, scented candles were spread all over the sophisticated, classical wooden furniture. There were torches hanging from the walls; the dream-like atmosphere was impossible to resist.

Dressed in a black coat adorned with a golden collar, Dr. Alonso crossed the room to greet him. "Welcome to our family, Thomas. Look around. We are the Orphics."

Several people dressed in white, silk tunics, softly swirled to the sound of a harp skillfully played by very beautiful young people. Some of them stopped and bowed as they noticed Thomas watching.

Delicious dishes were placed on the table with plenty of grapes, chestnuts, apples and, of course, bottles of red wine. A deep longing to belong to a family took over his heart, and all Thomas could say was, "Thank you, sir."

SINGING A PRAYER
UNDER THE STARS

Marlui knew the tracks that lead to the meadow by heart. She raced through the trees she had revered ever since she was a little girl, guided by the owls' hoots, her dogs barking alongside her.

There he was: Popygua. Marlui heaved a sigh of relief when she found her grandpa standing with his wooden guitar, singing out loud under the stars. She greeted him, but he did not answer her, nor acknowledge her presence. Marlui knew he was entranced. She would not be able to join him now that the singing had already begun.

She hoped Popygua was singing on Thomas's behalf. She tried to grasp the meaning of the words but couldn't. For the first time, Marlui deeply regretted never having taken the time to learn the ancient, secret, healing songs. *It's never too late*, she thought.

Marlui lay down on the leaves in the heart of the meadow, facing the sky. She noticed birds crossing the air, she heard foxes running close, and she saw huge bats silently crossing branches. She listened to her grandpa's lyrical prayer attentively. Slowly, the words seemed to make sense . . .

"Orpheus with his lute made trees"
BY WILLIAM SHAKESPEARE
(from Henry VIII)

Orpheus with his lute made trees,
And the mountain tops that freeze,
Bow themselves when he did sing:
To his music plants and flowers
Ever sprung; as sun and showers
There was a lasting spring.
Everything that heard him play,
Even the billows of the sea,
Hung their heads, and then lay by.
In sweet music is such art,
Killing care and grief of heart
Fall asleep, or hearing, die.

A TOAST TO ORPHEUS

Thomas was invited to take his seat at the dinner table. The words of Shakespeare's poem, interpreted by the lovely girl playing the harp, seemed to enhance the beauty all around him. As she finished reciting the last verse, everyone clapped, Thomas the most enthusiastically.

"A toast to Orpheus!" said Dr. Alonso, raising his crystal glass.

Thomas put the linen napkin on his lap and opened his mouth to speak. He wanted to thank Dr. Alonso for this memorable dinner. He was also curious about this Orphic society and its members. When he was about to speak, Dr. Alonso stared at him.

At first, Thomas thought his features had changed due to some optical illusion. The combination of torches and candles seemed to imprint a new contour to his chiseled features. His mouth smirked instead of producing his usual, large, confident smile. Alonso slowly took off his glasses, and as he carefully placed them on the table, Thomas noticed Alonso's pupils were so enlarged—they reminded him of two still-water pools. Coldness quickly infiltrated his senses, and he could not speak or move, as if he was paralyzed by some primeval fear. The next sentence by Alonso just made his panic grow deeper and deeper.

"Nice to meet you, my young friend."

"Dr. Alonso? I'm sorry. I don't understand. I have been staying at your house for two days now. I mean, this is our third dinner together." Thomas's voice quivered as he forced the words from his mouth.

"We have met before, Thomas, long before tonight."

Was Alonso intoxicated? Thomas pushed the wine glass away. He didn't want to feel tipsy. He sensed some sort of underlying danger. Verses from his favorite poem, "El Desdichado," crossed his mind, although he dared not say them aloud. But then he realized the words did not belong to the original Nerval's classical work—but to his own poem, verses he had recreated that did not seem to make much sense anymore . . . as if his mind—his memories—were breaking apart:

> *I am a street-walking charcoal with a heart full of songs,*
> *The Duke of Aquitaine who tortures tertulias 'till boredom.*
> *My lonesome star unstuck has gone,*
> *A black hole from the sun—a star was born.*

Focusing on the present moment at the dinner party, Thomas looked at Dr. Alonso. "We first met at the square, don't you remember?"

"Oh, dear . . .Orpheus children . . . As naive as their father."

Completely at loss for words, Thomas just stared.

"As they say, one should keep their friends close and their enemies even closer. This is the real reason why I invented this Orpheus society."

Thomas leaned over the table, looking around, trying to break the power of Alonso's commanding eyes.

"I must say, I am very fond of my host, Dr. Alonso."

A shiver ran down his spine. "What do you mean? Why did you say *host*?"

"My dear boy, Dr. Alonso has hosted my visits for years now. He has become such a dear friend of mine."

"Who are you?" Thomas asked the question and immediately

regretted it. Was he speaking to a mad person, or did Dr. Alonso have multiple personality disorder? As much as he wanted to leave the table and get out of the house as fast as he could, he couldn't resist waiting to hear the answer.

"I am Hades, the lord of the underworld and the ruler of Death. As I said, we have met long before this day. When we last met, you were a cute little boy, and I promised myself I would rescue you from the pain of living very soon. However, my enemies got to you before I could complete my plan."

Overwhelmed and shocked, all Thomas could manage to say was, "Enemies?"

"Oh, yes, my boy . . . They are numerous . . . Hermes, the traveling god, being the most notorious of them all, rescuing souls from my realm through the power of his enchanted words. However, this is not what happened to you. Your beautiful face caught the attention of my most powerful foe: Menomise, the muse of memory. I can never vanquish the power of memory to bring back to life souls I have already taken and brought to my world, and I had to win over Orpheus and his music too. It inspired people to love life. Besides, Orpheus could control all my monstrous creatures, the hell keepers, with the power of his music. So, I had to break him, and I did it. I played a trick on him. I forced him into a deal I knew he would not be able to win. I knew he did not trust me. I knew he would look back to check if his beloved Euridice was following him out of my domain. He lost, and she was kept with me forever, leading Orpheus to lose his will to live. He blamed himself, becoming but a dead shadow, until he finally left the world of the living. Of course, Zeus knew of my ruse and would not allow me to have Orpheus with me, so he was turned into a Constellation.

To make a long story short, I should have taken you along with your parents. Don't you remember our meeting? At night? At the accident? Inside the car? You were so little, and you could already sense my presence. You even greeted me . . . You were crying, so I told you I would come back for you in no time."

"You mean that you are going to kill me now?" Thomas asked bluntly.

"If I were to take you now, my dear host, Dr. Alonso, might be accused of murder. Besides, there are worse things than a good death."

Hades stood up as he finished his sentence, and Thomas felt as if he were encapsulated in a freezing time warp. He couldn't leave the table or run out of the house. So, he asked, "What could be worse than dying?"

"Ah, my boy, it is so obvious, can't you see? Betraying one's true self. As Orpheus could not trust his Euridice's true love, I can always instill mistrust into a person's heart, so they won't listen or abide by their true desires. They follow the crowd. They start making choices out of fear or the wish to please others. They cannot put up with the smallest frustrations. They hate to struggle for what they really want. Now, a true desire is a light guide through one's life path. It so happens that several times, truthful desires don't comply with common sense nor conventions. Denial of one's intimate, secret dream is the fastest way to emptiness. Hollow people give up on their souls so easily, my boy. You are not entirely hollow, of course, but you don't truly follow your inner desires either. You don't know what you truly want. You choose what seems more appropriate, conventional, and easier in the moment. So, it will not be too hard for me to take your soul away, whilst leaving your body behind. You will never go back to your senses, and you will never be able to honor my rival, Orpheus, with your outstanding musical skills . . . You will no longer love or create, and most of all, you will stop spreading happiness around. Happy people don't want to die. You make it difficult for me to get ahold of their souls "I will be undead?" Thomas looked around; all he could see now was the long, black table and Hades' piercing gaze. Memories from the fatal accident that took away his family flashed through his mind. A deep death wish lurked within him, and he felt a longing desire to be with his father and mother once more.

SAD LULLABY

Gabriella held her little son and tried to understand his sinister humming. His face was wet with tears as he sat on the carpet, legs crossed, and rocked his body. The colorful furniture, the fluffy carpet, the toys over the shelves—no matter how cozy the kids' rooms seemed to look, a feeling of uneasiness threw shadows over both their parents' hearts.

"Oh, dear, what can we do? André seems to be deep in some kind of nightmare."

Jonas sat behind Gabriella, holding both his wife and son tightly. Tears wet his face as he realized he had no idea what to do.

"Let me sing to him," said Manuel.

Guilt flowed through Gabriella. They had left their youngest son out of their embrace. So concerned and frightened over André's haunted melody, they'd forgotten about him.

"Come here, my dear," Gabriella said to her little boy.

Jonas left the three-party embrace. "Yes, join with us, Manuel. So sorry. I should have hugged you too."

"Mom, just let me sing," said Manuel. "Can't you hear her voice?"

"Whose voice?" asked Gabriella.

"Marlui's voice. She is singing along . . ."

Gabriella dared not say a word. She inhaled deeply, and the scent of fresh leaves and flowers filled her nostrils. She closed her eyes and hoped her tiny little boy could sing his older brother out of his nightmare . . .

STAR SOUL

"Don't you feel like a stranger on this Earth, Thomas?"
Dr. Alonso's questions, now acting as Hades' mouthpiece, were relentless. "Don't you feel as if you have never truly embraced human life, my boy?"

Thomas tried to move out of his chair but could not. Perplexity and fear seemed to keep him stuck to that dinner table, among the strangest people he had ever met, lost in the most frightening scenario he had ever faced. Now, the swaying people in silk did not look so beautiful anymore, their faces pale and their smiles sad and fake. Not only Dr. Alonso's face had changed, but it appeared all the guests were actually hosting creatures from hell.

Hades would not stop talking. "Artists are forever longing to return to their original homeland in the stars. They need to leave this life and be close to Orpheus's constellation, their everlasting source of inspiration. It is as if they were torn between the task of triggering the wish to live fully in other people's hearts and their own secret—a silent death wish. Hence their attraction to me . . ."

"Attraction to you?" Thomas was so outraged by Hades' reasoning; he could not avoid questioning his words.

"As I already said, we have met before, my dear young man . . ."

"Yes, at the square!"

"No, there were previous meetings with me, as you know."

Thomas stared at the face of the man he knew as Dr. Alonso and barely recognized it. The cruel smirk, magnetic eyes, and the hollow voice did not belong to him. Dr. Alonso was no longer there—he knew it for sure now.

"Did you think you were seduced by the beautiful Dora? Is this why you came?" asked Hades. "Was Dora the only reason why you accepted our invitation to come, or was it the lute? Just close your eyes and try to remember me . . . That night, in the car . . . come with me and join your parents in my underworld. Don't you miss them at all?"

"Enough!" said Thomas, and he rose from the table. "I want to leave NOW! Enough of this stupid masquerade! Carnival is over, you know!"

All of sudden, Dr. Alonso's voice was back to his own mouth. His large, cheerful smile spread all over his face again as Dora approached swiftly and kissed Thomas on the face.

"Please, don't take me the wrong way," said Dr. Alonso. "I am just referring to the orphic myths. You see, according to the old, secret scriptures, human souls dwelled upon the stars. From there, every soul that fell on earth had to associate with a human body. Some privileged souls, such as yourself, keep the original spark of their starry homes. No wonder most artists would rather work at night, composing, writing, entertaining . . ."

"Stop with this esoteric mumbo jumbo," Thomas shouted, pushing Dora away. "I want to leave this mad house, this ship of fools. You are nothing but a bunch of ridiculous, snobbish, boring, shallow people spending their time and money trying to convince yourselves that you are special. You are not above average; you are below everything."

"Father is not a loser," screamed Dora, her eyes full of angry tears. She pointed at a pedestal in the center of the room. "An authentic Greek fifth-century bone tablet. Just look at the inscriptions. Please, take a look, Thomas, and you will know we are not just a bunch of posh posers. Our research, our knowledge, is deep."

LIFE. DEATH. TRUTH.

As Thomas read the words inscribed on the ancient bone tablet, a strange and unexpected need to know more about this piece took over his senses.

Dora quickly perceived his hesitation and gave him a guitar. "Read the words and play, Thomas. Just play. Do it now. I won't take no for an answer."

Slowly, looking down, Thomas sat back at the table, took his guitar, and just played . . .

THE PROMISE

"Can't believe they have finally fallen asleep," Jonas said as he came into the bedroom.

"I am still deeply worried," Gabriella said.

Jonas sat by the bed and slowly took off his sleepers. Gabriella noticed the tension in his shoulders and hugged him tenderly. "Let me give you a massage." Her hands traced the skin on his back, kneading and working the tension out of the tense muscles. "The boys seem to have a strange connection with Thomas. They dreamt about him; they knew his songs a week before they actually met him at the fountain. Please, don't tell me it is just my writer's imagination speaking. I'm talking as their mother. You witnessed this phenomenon yourself, and I really don't think it's all a random coincidence."

Jonas took her right hand and kissed it. "Thank you. Your hands always work their magic. My shoulders have been so tense, and yes, I understand what you are saying, and I hear you. My intuition tells me the boys are connecting to Thomas in some way and acting out some of his troubles. I have a feeling that he's not very well at the moment and that we have to rescue him. I know it sounds crazy, but I really do feel this is something we have to do."

Jonas gave Gabriella a brief kiss before he lay back and crossed his hands over his chest. He usually did this when he needed to think. "Where is his family? Why did he submit so easily to Alonso?"

Gabriella rolled over on her side to face him. "I have been

researching Thomas on the internet. Apparently, he lost his family in a car accident. Being born into wealth, he was looked after by tutors. Both his parents were only children, so he doesn't have any relatives. He sounds a bit like a lonely rich boy. However, he has lived a good life; he is a very creative and prestigious young musician. But as far as his personal life is concerned, he is more of a loner. It took me a while to find him on social media, so he doesn't rely on that."

Jonas turned off the light. "Being an orphan is not easy. There are so many emotional distortions such a loss can produce. And orphan status is not exclusive to those who've lost their parents. There are many ways for an adolescent to disconnect from their family. Being emotionally torn away from one's home can be a heavy toll. Remember when I was working with the kids in the juvenile prison?"

Gabriella looked lovingly at Jonas's profile against the shadows and stroked his hair while he spoke.

"I had been invited by the psychologist's team to work with the children. All I had to do was teach them how to draw a house. So many of those kids just couldn't picture themselves inside homes, or any conventional buildings, to be honest. They only wanted to draw streets, dead ends, alleys, squares. They didn't seem to care much for nature or open spaces . . . Anyway, I could tell the ones who were really bonding with me because they became either aggressive or aloof. Some of my best students quit the class. I couldn't figure it out until my supervisor told me that some of the kids couldn't bear the intensity of bonding. They were terrified of rejection, so they would rather leave, when things were still good."

"That's good to know. I'll keep it in mind," Gabriella said.

She nodded and yawned, and he went on. "I promise you, we'll rescue Thomas. Even if we have to make fools out of ourselves.

There's just one more thing before you fall asleep. What about Marlui? Why did the boys say they could hear her voice?"

"I haven't a clue. But I'm going to call her first thing in the morning. I didn't tell you, but I could hear her voice as well, or at least I thought I could. It all felt a bit like a strange dream."

"It does feel a bit like a dream, but we'll figure it out. But not without a good night's sleep."

LIFE IS TRUTH

Thomas played a melody, the huge letters on the pedestal calling to him. Those three words seemed to summon his deepest nostalgia and pull it to the surface.

LIFE. TRUTH. DEATH.

He changed the dynamics to introduce the melody of a traditional child's song his mother used to hum when she tucked him into bed. Thomas closed his eyes, and an intricate constellation of needs, pains, and losses found their way into his wounded heart. He remembered sitting in the back of the crashed car, wanting to rescue his dying parents, then the sharp pain of isolation as he left the hospital and moved back to his house alone.

The word *death* gave way to *truth*, and he swiftly experienced the memories of the dance of his secret sound friends. He played joyfully now, to call their attention, the need for their company stinging his aching heart. They didn't come. As much as he called their melodic voices, performing songs they had shared with him, they still remained absent.

"What is life, anyway?" Thomas asked himself, and rageful instincts took over his fingers as he moved his song to an entirely new rhythm. He tapped the body of the guitar. He tapped his feet. He shook his long hair wildly. He sang.He wanted to leave this life and join the stars—forever part of a constellation. Far from the maddening crowd. He tried to stop, to breathe deeply and move on to another melody, to a new mood, but he couldn't. He looked around at the audience quietly staring at him, as if cruelly waiting for the moment he would collapse and be gone.

"How could they share such a dreadful desire? Do I wish to die? Is it nothing but my own deepest desire? To perish? Here? Now?"

EARTH SKY

"Spread the sky roots, my child. Now. Sing along. Let's reach Thomas. Let your spirit travel along with mine."

Popygua's words echoed through the trees, followed by owls hooting and monkeys' noisy movements jumping over the treetops. He looked at the stars and beseeched his gods to help him heal and rescue a young life about to be taken away. Then he sang.

Marlui opened up her arms and legs over the soft, green grass. She looked up at the sparkling stars against the sky and sang along with the sacred song. At each praying verse, she felt the extremities from her body stretching more and more until they seemed to reach all across the meadow. Her fingers, arms, legs, feet, and hair sunk into the earth as she selflessly let her own body become roots entangled so strongly with the earth that nothing and no one would be able to pluck her out of there.

"Thomas. Listen. Just hear our song," she cried.

THE LAST SONG

Margaret left the back of the room and walked toward Thomas. "Why had he not fainted? Why had he not passed away right there so that the entire audience could dance around his motionless body? The ritual is infallible," she thought.

She approached the pedestal, forcing her way through the happily dancing bodies. "What is this?" she asked herself. Then she heard the magic in the young man's music. A kissing couple stumbled over her and almost knocked her to the floor, completely oblivious to anything but their romance. A myriad of mixed emotions crossed her heart—anger, fear, jealousy—and finally, she was overcome by sudden, poignant memories of her first kisses as a young woman. Her body felt strong, young, yearning for love, and all she wanted to do was swirl around the hall led by the shifting melodies the young musician played.

Thomas looked around him and saw girls letting their hair loose from their Greek hairstyles. He noticed the people in white, silk costumes sitting on the floor, laughing. There were people hugging each other like little kids. He felt his own heart open to new melodies and instinctively searched for his own childhood secret creatures of sound. There they were. Surrounding him, once again.

Dora looked at Thomas, and he had changed the rhythm of his song again. Eyes closed, he seemed to be transported to another realm, a very secretive place of his own. She knew she had to call her father. Where was he? Someone had to record the music, because she knew Thomas would never be able to play that well again. It was always the same routine. Her father's rites put these young talented men in their best creative state, just to register their musical peak. She heaved deeply, feeling so sorry for Thomas and so ashamed of herself for having brought him there, into her father's malignant trap. Waves of deep affection for Thomas overwhelmed her as she witnessed the sheer joy and happiness imprinted on people's faces. Why could she never follow her own instincts? Why did she have to continually please her father, knowing that his wishes were endlessly selfish? Revolt overtook her as she saw her father approaching with his camera. He'd never be able to take part in the joy unless he was the one to record it, to possess the beautiful moment. She ran toward him, wanting to grab the camera. She wanted to push him out of the enchanted circle that Thomas had created. She wanted to protect Thomas at all costs, realizing he had won her heart like no other boy had ever been able to do.

As she ran, she felt different, a happy little girl who only wanted to dance and lose herself among all the others in the room. Freedom and merriment engulfed her, and a song burst from her lips. It deflected her from facing her father.

Panic, horror, dismay. Thomas couldn't describe the feelings that flooded his body when he saw Dr. Alonso and his camera, capturing his face as if he could steal his soul away. Something seemed to dissolve inside of him as he noticed his secret sound creatures abandoning him once more. He stopped playing, hands paralyzed by a stinging sense of doom. He felt so old and worn now. People were still dancing like he had mesmerized them forever, but his hands could no longer move. He knew he had just performed his last song. The best in his entire life. It didn't bring him any joy. Thomas felt defeated—deprived of his youth.

Totally indifferent to his pain, the crowd called for an encore. People cheered and clapped their hands. Others held each other and continued dancing. They were not ready to let him go. They wanted more.

"Go on, Thomas, don't stop now! I need to catch you on film," screamed Dr. Alonso.

Thomas looked back at the audience, trying to connect to them, to seize what they were feeling, to recapture his own song, now entangled in their memories. He couldn't disobey Dr. Alonso's command. Or was it Hades' orders?

Thomas felt weak and dizzy, his heart was beating desperately; it felt like his life force was leaving his body. A gust of wind blew the windows wide open, and the scent of dewy leaves and running water reached Thomas's nostrils. He closed his eyes in an attempt to inhale their natural fragrance. Then he heard it, the songs of speaking trees, the voices of nocturnal animals, and the chirping of night birds producing such a fresh melody. He had to play it. He took hold of his guitar once more and let his music channel the voices of the forest; he felt his heart fill with so many new stories to share.

He could hear Marlui and Popygua's sacred songs all around him, like some sort of invincible shield of beauty. His body began to relax. Thomas smiled and stared right into Dr. Alonso's eyes as he played the new tune.

Dr. Alonso took a step toward Thomas, the camera slipping from his hands. He felt invigorated as he began to whistle. He took a seat next to Thomas and whistled so perfectly—he sounded as if he were a magical, timeless instrument. Their duet quickly brought the crowd together. Tender hugs and kisses were exchanged, and sweet dreams filled everyone's imagination.

Dora looked at her father's face, the tears streaming down his cheeks. She forgave herself for always wanting to please him. He was free now, and she knew her father would always be himself. No more arrogant professor and no more a voice for Hades. The talented boy he'd once been had awoken once more and stepped forward to reveal a new path.

She looked at her mother, Margaret, and they hugged each other tenderly. She looked at her reflection in the large hall mirror, and at first, she couldn't recognize the smiling girl staring back. Her beauty shone from within. Her joy was raw, almost brutal, and totally invigorating.

RECONNECTION

"Hello. I'm so glad you've come. I had the most horrendous night's sleep. I knew I'd have the worst nightmares if I tried to close my eyes, so I kept them open. It's strange. I'm not tired, though. If anything, I'm excited. I can't wait to barge into Dr. Alonso's little palace."

Vera couldn't stop talking. She'd been waiting for her friends at the bench in the square for over an hour. Her heart skipped a beat when she saw André and Manuel running toward her, followed closely by Gabriella and Jonas.

"I hope you don't mind us bringing the kids," Gabriella said, leaning in to kiss Vera on the cheek.

"They woke at the crack of dawn, and all they wanted to do was go and find their friend Thomas," Jonas added.

The adults sat on the bench while the boys played with their crazy toys. Jonas couldn't stop himself from teasing Vera. "Of all the people, not even in my wildest dreams would I have imagined being here with you, Vera, let alone joining a rescue party for a boy I've never met."

Gabriella laughed. "I must confess this whole rescue scenario seems more exciting than any action plot I could come up with in my writing. What's the plan? I'm dying to know."

André and Miguel came running toward them, ice cream in hands, and stopped in front of Gabriella. "Where's Marlui?"

Gabriella immediately excused herself. "Sorry, guys. We'll

have to wait for Marlui before you explain your plan."

Vera nodded and smiled. "She is on her way. She just texted me. I think I'll grab an ice cream as well while we wait. You know, ever since our first meeting, here on the square, I feel as if I've drank water from a magical fountain of youth. I feel as if I am changing so fast . . . It's hard to explain."

Jonas cleared his throat. "I have felt the same. Vera, I guess you and I belong to the same species of rational beings. I haven't found rational explanations for having joined this crazy rescue party either."

Gabriella caressed her husband's shoulders. He seemed so at ease among these people they hardly knew.

Jonas stood up and stretched his long legs. "Vera and I have been friends for years now. Yes, we work together, but we have developed a deep bond, even though we are not like-minded, not at all. I love myths, literature, and cinema, and Vera is my grounder, so to speak, always bringing me down to earth. However, this time, I think it is the other way around."

Vera placed a hand on Jonas's arm, offering a sincere smile. "My father was a renowned lawyer. My mother was this dreamy, beautiful woman obsessed with ancient rites and magic. I was their only child. Unfortunately, my father passed away too soon. I was only nine. I idolized him. We loved to read encyclopedias together and biographies. He taught me about law from a very early age. I was never interested in my mother's research. I never even enjoyed fairy tales, you see. . ."She paused and looked at the trees.

Gabriella noticed Vera's eyes were welling with tears. "An only child who is cut away from her favorite parent . . . I guess you and Thomas have something in common. Is it the reason why you are going out of your way to help him?"

Vera was speechless, and before she got the chance to reply,

Jonas spoke up. "If I'm honest, I'm not here for Thomas. I looked him up online, and yes, his music is amazing, but my true intention in all this is to expose Dr. Alonso's madness to the world. I will sue him if I can. He has to be stopped, and that's why I'm here."

Gabriella realized Vera and her husband really meant what they said. Dr. Alonso had two very dangerous adversaries in them.

Vera sat back down. "Thomas's music . . .there is a magical element to it. By listening to his melodies, I suddenly understood my mother's interest in the occult. Where do his songs come from? Does he tap into some secret musical source? I must say, he has transported me to other realms, as my late mother would say. Fact is, this whole Thomas situation has helped me reconnect with my mother's memories and love, even though she has been gone for a while now. I don't usually confide in strangers, but there is something I feel I need to tell you."

Gabriella placed a hand on Vera's and urged her to continue. "When my father passed, I couldn't move past my grief. My mom kept on telling me he wasn't really gone, that my father would always be by my side. I hated her for it. I just wanted him back, in the flesh. But when I sat here by the fountain, listening to Thomas's music, I felt my father's presence. So, I spent last night reading my mother's books on ancient magic. For the first time, I realized there was a grain of truth in her research, even if only metaphorically. I have always focused on the raw side of life. I mean, I interpret reality differently than her views, if you know what I mean."

Gabriella hugged Vera, a deep affection moving her body toward her new friend, when the boys happily announced that Marlui had arrived. They ran toward the young woman, who immediately kneeled to hug and kiss them.

"Hello, guys. I am so glad you are all here. We must hurry. Thomas is in danger."

Vera sat up straight. "Has he called you? Has he texted you, Marlui? Or is it just a gut feeling or weird vision, a nightmare of yours? Has he actually spoken to you, Marlui? I must say I am not a spiritual person. I don't believe in superstition! I need facts!"

Marlui's eyes were moist, and she touched her belly as if she had been punched. Then, slowly, she took a seat on the bench and turned toward Vera. "Our ancient traditions should not be reduced and seen as primitive peoples' superstitions! Vera, I don't like to say it, but either you respect my ways, or I will try and solve this whole thing by myself. I am so tired of your passive-aggressive comments. My people's laws never had to be documented because we have always relied on the spoken word. We believe that you—who call yourselves "civilized" because you rely mainly on written words and data—lack the deep commitment with truth which is evident in our culture. Likewise, the fact that we have only now started to register our traditional wisdom into books does not diminish its value. On the contrary, we believe our sensitivity and our healing tools should only be transmitted from mouth to ear. Orally, I mean, and only to the ones who will not misuse our sacred knowledge."

"Marlui, I am so sorry. You see, I don't think I will ever trust spoken words more than I trust written laws. I will never trust intuition more than I trust Cartesian reasoning, but I see your point. I promise, in my mother's name, I will follow you, no matter your decision-making method."

Marlui left her seat and hugged Vera.

"I truly wish you had met my mother," said Vera.

"I am sure I would have loved her, Vera. Thanks for being such a true friend."

Jonas smiled at both of them. "We have to move on. Time is running out. We can use our van so we can all stay together, but I think we should leave now."

BLACK COFFEE

Thomas woke up and tried to remember the previous night's events. For a few seconds, he rejoiced at his success. He thought about how much he had enjoyed the sensation of liberating the family, Dr. Alonso, Margaret, and Dora from their inner traps and traumas.

He looked at his guitar and luggage sitting by the wall and decided the time had come for him to leave. He should pack before breakfast, share his last meal with his hosts, thank them for the hospitality, and leave. He longed to be back home. Yet, as he sat on the bed, Thomas was aware of a deep fatigue. "Why am I so very tired?" He decided to take a shower to renew his energy. Not even the pleasantness of warm water over his head seemed to do him any good. Just the opposite. Running water over his back had brought with it the memory of painful tears. He would not allow himself to cry, though. Not at that moment. All he had to do was leave, and all these uncanny feelings would dissipate.

Thomas quickly put on the same clothes he arrived in, combed his wet hair, and did not shave. Somehow, he could not face the mirror. Leaving his luggage and guitar all set to go, he went into the dining room.

As he stepped into the hall, Dr. Alonso greeted him. "Bravo. You gave us a mesmerizing presentation last night."

Margaret clapped her hands, and so did Dora, as if Thomas was still finishing his music on the stage. Thomas didn't know what to say. He looked down at his feet, rather awkwardly, and slowly took his seat at the table. The maid offered him some black coffee. Thomas swallowed his first cup very fast, trying to wake himself up, to feel lively and happy as he normally did every single morning. No. His fatigue was overwhelming. He asked for three more cups of strong coffee and drank them in no time. But when he wanted some more, Margaret intervened.

"Are you sure you want a fourth espresso, Thomas? Sorry for intruding, but that's about a liter of very strong black coffee. I know I sound motherly, Thomas, but I am so very grateful to you. I have no words to describe all the joy your music brought to this family last night. I just can't believe Alonso is whistling again. I haven't heard him do that since we were first in love."

Thomas insisted on one more cup of black coffee. Dr. Alonso kept on chatting with his wife and daughter, his features shining with such youthful joy. As for Dora, yes, Dora . . .she was more beautiful than ever—sleek, sophisticated, and lighthearted, in a seductive way.

She tried to hold Thomas's hand over the table, but he instinctively deflected from her caress.

"What's the matter, Thomas? We love you so much now," she said, smiling sweetly.

Thomas saw his reflection in the wide mirror across the wall and noticed huge, black circles around his eyes. His skin was pale and dry, his lips white. "I am afraid I must go home now. Thank you for the delicious meal, but I still feel weak and dizzy. I must be getting the flu, and I don't want to pass it on to any of you. Could you please call a cab for me, Dora?"

Dora's facial expression immediately changed from a happy, lighthearted girl to a bitter, possessive young woman. "No!" she said bluntly, rising from the table. "You cannot leave us now."

"I am not leaving you. I just want to go home and get some sleep," argued Thomas.

"Yes, you must stay here, with us," said Margaret. Then she added, "We can provide for all your needs, Thomas. We can put you in a very comfortable room, call a doctor friend of ours. We shall do whatever it takes for you to stay here, with us."

Thomas rose from the table, nausea coursing through his body. "Thank you for your kindness. I appreciate it, but I really must go. I have already packed, you see? All I need is to take a cab home."

Dr. Alonso swiftly left the table and walked toward the lute hanging on the wall by the pedestal. "Take it, Thomas. Don't you want to develop your songs into an actual historical instrument?"

Thomas walked toward his room to get his guitar and suitcase, but Dr. Alonso called after him, "Wait, Thomas. You cannot leave us. You must stay with us. You are like a son to me now."

Turning on his heels, Thomas struggled to get the words out. "Why on earth do you want me to stay? Last night, you were celebrating your own freedom. Why do you want to make me your prisoner? I don't understand. Aren't you free from your inhibitions, traumas, toxic memories, whatever? Why do you keep on asking for more and more and more?"

Dr. Alonso put himself in between Thomas and the corridor entrance. Margaret stood by his side, arms crossed, her eyes furious. "You see, Thomas," said Dr. Alonso, "that is the irony of this whole situation. We can only feel free if you keep on playing your guitar for us, if you keep on releasing us from ourselves. Being ours, you will definitely keep on setting us free. And you won't feel like you're in a prison. We shall throw parties daily. You will play with amazing instruments and enjoy the best cuisine. Besides, I want to share my library with you, my secret teachings. You will be truly powerful, Thomas, as no one else before you."

Dora took a step forward and stared into Thomas's eyes. "Father, leave him be. He doesn't deserve being here with us."

Thomas was shocked. Dora's eyes seemed haughty, cruelly cold. But he did not hesitate nor thank her. Without saying a word, or kissing her goodbye, he left behind his luggage and guitar and walked out of the house. As he reached the open road, he started running blindly. The road took a turn, and when he ran through its curve, he looked back. No one was following him. The house was finally out of sight. Even so, Thomas just kept on running, his breath flowing strongly and his heart racing.

ON THE ROAD

"Thomas is coming!" said Marlui from the back seat of the van.

"Ah, there she goes again. Our beautiful seer," said Vera. "I am sorry, but you must be wrong. My GPS says we still have fifteen minutes to go."

Marlui closed her eyes. "He is coming. I can see him."

"Oh, dear," said Vera, "please, don't tell me you can see with your eyes closed."

Jonas decided to intervene, changing the subject. "By the way, Vera, don't you think our plan is kind of lame? Will Dr. Alonso open the gates for us just because we are bringing him a rare book on magic? I hardly speak to him at the campus. I don't really like him, so I try to avoid him by all means."

André and Manuel sat in the back seat and caressed Marlui's soft hair. "He is coming. Thomas is coming to us."

Gabriella smiled at her boys. "You can use me as an excuse. I brought my camera as well. We can tell him we want to make a documentary about him."

Jonas smiled at his wife. "Without having set an appointment? It would still sound very lame."

"We must take our chances," said Vera. "If he is as obsessed with magic as my mother was, he will open the gates to his house as soon as I mention the title of the book."

Gabriella leaned toward the driver's seat. "Please tell me more about the book. I am dying of curiosity now."

Vera took a look at her GPS and mumbled, "Ten minutes to go." Then she said, "*The Emerald Tablet*, my mother's favorite edition."

"That's a beautiful title. What's it about? Is it a novel of some sort?"

"It's a very mysterious book. According to legend, it was written by Hermes Trismegistus, a Hellenic mythical character. It is considered the foundational text of European alchemy and has some connection to the search for the philosopher's stone. Its oldest versions date back to the late eighth century. It was very popular in the nineteenth century, and this particular edition belonged to a famous occultist, which is what will really grab Dr. Alonso's attention. 'As above, so below,' became a motto during the twentieth century, when my mother was still a young, lovely woman. I can remember her quoting the sentence out of nothing."

"Thomas," screamed both boys at the same time. "Look! He is there, by the road."

Vera smiled to herself. *Mom would have loved to be with me now, partaking in this mad adventure,* she thought. There he was, Thomas! Sitting by the road. She parked Jonas's van and turned back to tell Marlui that yes, she had been right all the time, but the girl was already getting out of the vehicle. Vera heaved a sigh of relief as she saw the boys and Marlui holding Thomas. Apart from the fact that he seemed very tired, everything seemed to be all right with him.

OUT OF WORDS

"Are you all right?" asked Jonas, crouching by Thomas at the side of the road.

Manuel and André were holding his shaking shoulders. Marlui caressed Thomas's hair, but he would not lift his eyes. Gabriella and Jonas addressed him as well. "Hello, again, Thomas. We came here to rescue you."

Jonas was startled. There was something off about the young man. Not only was he out of words, but he seemed fragile, skinny, pale, like someone who had just faced a terrible disease. He could not stop himself from saying, "I am so glad you are well, sane, and alive, my friend. I swear I will sue that psychopath. Dr. Alonso cannot keep on damaging the likes of you. He has already traumatized two students of mine."

Marlui placed her fingers to her lips, asking for silence. As she tried to soothe Thomas, he started sobbing violently. His body shivering, he seemed to be lost and lonely. All of them, Vera included, opened their arms to hold him tenderly.

Marlui kissed him on the cheek and helped him rise from the road. "Time to come home, Thomas. Let's just get out of here," she said.

Thomas looked around him, regaining consciousness after a long, dangerous nightmare, and he followed his new friends to their van.

As Gabriella opened the door to her boys, they turned to

Thomas. "We will sing for you on the way home. You will feel good, we know."

Thomas tossed his long hair back and straightened up his shoulders with a faint smile. "Thank you all," he said. "I am not sure what has happened to me during the last few days. I must think it all over. My mind seems to be playing tricks on me. I cannot trust myself, you see? All my memories seem to be enshrouded by crazy dreams. I cannot distinguish truth from illusion. But I do have an actual, down-to-earth question for you. Do you, by any chance, have my address?"

Jonas laughed out loud. "We don't know where you live. Isn't this a weird situation? Here we are, acting as your lifetime friends, but the fact is, we know so little about you."

Gabriella addressed Thomas, "Why don't you come to our house for some coffee and cake? We must get to know each other on a more regular basis. Our house is very cozy, I assure you. Besides, we do want to spend some more time with you now."

André and Manuel started jumping on the back seat and insisting he agree. André said, "Yes, Thomas, please come to our house."

"Please come," Manuel added. "We want to show you our toys. We even have a new gift for you."

Tiredness, tension, and fatigue seemed to diminish as Thomas smiled and nodded, accepting their invitation.

THE DANCING SPIRITS

Thomas did not want to leave the kids.

Sitting over a comfy orange couch, surrounded by the craziest handcrafted toys he had ever seen, he kept on wishing he too had experienced such a joyful childhood as these two little brothers.

Manuel and André moved around their bedroom, picking up pieces of old toys from a large, wooden truck. "This trunk belonged to our granny. She gave it to us, and Mom thought it should be a good place to keep our useless, broken toys. We just hate to throw them away, so we just toss them here. Whenever we want to invent new toys, we can choose from these pieces. It is so much more fun than new toys."

Thomas laughed, feeling deep comfort. As he heard his own laughter, he realized the painful feeling of hollowness finally leaving his chest. "Can I join you, guys?"

Marlui approached, sitting beside Thomas on the couch. She hugged him. "You seem so much better now, Thomas."

He looked down, overwhelmed by shyness and a sudden, piercing feeling of happiness. Marlui sensed it and let go of him. "I'm sorry, Thomas. I feel as if I have known you all my life. Don't take me for some invasive groupie, stepping over your boundaries."

Thomas did not find words to reply, so he just hugged Marlui for a long time and whispered in her ear, "Thank you."

When he looked back at the boys, he saw them, his secret

creatures of sound. "Oh, wow," he mumbled, then he tried to act naturally, pretending he was not seeing anything special.

"The dancing spirits . . . yes, they are here now," said Marlui, smiling as well.

Thomas could not believe his ears. He turned to Marlui. "Can you see them? I mean, can your eyes capture these beautiful dancing shapes? Can you hear their music?"

Marlui took his hands, kissed Thomas on the cheeks, and said, "Of course, I can. I have seen them since I was a little girl. But this is the first time I've seen them around urban kids. Of course, I saw them floating around you, when I saw you play, at the square."

"Tell me, what are they? I have always loved their music."

"Grandpa says they come from the *sacred tree of life*. The sacred tree roots spread all over the planet, and their leaves reach over all places and times. We revere the forest, you know. Trees are holy to us. The fact is, I believe trees, forests, and their creatures should be loved by all. We, humans, belong to the forest as much as all other living beings. If people could realize that, if we all could enjoy the music of nature, the world would be a better place, I am sure."

Manuel and André started humming a lovely song, echoing the melody whispered by the secret creatures of sound.

Marlui caressed Thomas's soft hair and stared into his eyes. "These two cute boys have been chosen . . . just like you, Thomas. I am sure you have sensed the dancing spirit's presence since you were very young. Unlike so many children, you understood their musical language; you learned to channel their voices so that everyone would be able to enjoy them. You have always been such a generous soul. I really love you, Thomas . . ."

Thomas could not believe her words, how unexpected they were, so out of the blue. He smiled, pleasantly surprised, and was about to say something, but Jonas came into their kid's bedroom. Marlui and Thomas were sitting on the carpet. He waited a few seconds before calling everyone to dinner. There was something magical about the whole scene, as if a timeless enchantment had enveloped his kids, beautiful Marlui, and Thomas. Jonas certainly did not want to break the spell.

"Dinner is ready," shouted Gabriella.

Marlui whispered to Thomas. "Grandpa wants to speak to you, Thomas."

Thomas smiled at her. "Of course, I would love to meet him!"

She laughed. "You have already met him… I will explain that to you later on. Now it's time for both of you to have a long conversation, face-to-face, I mean."

"Dinner is ready!" insisted Gabriella.

A few moments later, at the table, Thomas tried to answer Jonas's questions about Dr. Alonso and his secret cult. "They call themselves the Orphics. All their rites are connected to musical performances and historical relics. Apparently, Dr. Alonso is a collector of archaic instruments and music sheets. He is such a strange man. I got the impression he had multiple personality disorder. I don't really know because I am not a psychologist, and he was actually surrounded by several devoted disciples. For a few seconds, I actually believed he could see my past. Yet, now, with you, I realize he could have simply researched about my life on the internet. I might have been truly naive, but he did seem to control my mind during my stay there. And there is also Dora, his daughter."

Suddenly, Thomas stopped talking. He looked at Marlui as if feeling sorry for something. "I am so sorry, but I cannot give you more information right now. I need some time to myself. I can't really understand what happened there. I must sort it all out. My mind is a mess. Besides, I feel constantly weak, disoriented, depressed. I mean, I definitely need some time to think it all over. Right now, I would not be able to share with you all the things that happened while I stayed at Dr. Alonso's. I feel as if I'm not sure whether I really lived through it, or if it was mostly a nightmare. I feel out of my own mind, if you know what I mean."

Marlui sat by Thomas and thanked Gabriella for such a wonderful meal. "I am not sure about going after Dr. Alonso right now. I agree with Thomas. We must take our time and analyze Dr. Alonso's situation very carefully, not only because he looks like a dangerous, powerful man but because there are other things at stake. I assure you, there are other causes, very demanding ones, in fact, worth fighting for."

Jonas helped himself to some fresh salad. "Forest people preservation. Is that what you mean?"

"Well, I would like to invite all of you to spend some time in our community. I am sure you would have a great time with us."

André and Manuel immediately accepted her invitation, as well as Jonas and Gabriella. Vera pursed her lips. "I guess I will have to buy some sneakers. Please, don't laugh at me, Marlui. I am the typical urban lady, high heels and all."

Thomas smiled. "Can I meet him tomorrow?"

Marlui nodded at him, and to the rest, she said, "Guys, let's set a date for your visit. What about a week from now? I just need seven days."

"May I ask what you have in mind, dear Marlui? You see, unlike you, I am no mind reader . . .but, somehow, I am under the impression that Thomas has been invited to visit your house earlier than us. Am I right?" Vera asked.

Marlui nodded and turned to Thomas. "What about tonight, Thomas? Could you come and meet us?"

ARMADILLO RIDE

Driving along the open dirt road early in the morning felt so refreshing. Thomas took a deep breath and looked at Marlui by his side and smiled. Once again, he seemed to be lost for words. However, for the first time in years, he felt comfortable in silence. As a little boy, his parents used to take him out on long, quiet road trips. He had loved listening to his mother and remembered in the silence what she used to say.

"Look around you, my son. There is always so much beauty on the road: the trees, the clouds, lakes, the passing landscapes. Listen to life. We are just passengers, you know. Every road opens up space for inner journeys. Look at the road inside you, as well, my dear boy, and enjoy the ride."

He remembered then how the three of them—father, mother, and son—would quietly cross the endless country roads, exchanging a few words, some crackers, or a bottle of water. Thomas had traveled to distant places after their passing, but he kept on revering the road as a blessed place. Of course, he had met so many people who felt impatient when traveling, who would rather just keep their ears plugged or play some loud music along the way, singing along. Years later, as a musician on the road during his tours, he had friends that wouldn't stop chatting, and although Thomas wasn't confident enough to tell them he would much rather keep quiet, he never really did pay attention to their words. The road itself had so many stories to tell him.

He loved that Marlui seemed to understand the deep

eloquence of silence. She had declared her love for him, and he felt too overwhelmed to refer to that moment again. It did not seem to matter to her. There she was, simply by his side, no words, yet there was such depth of feelings. Marlui stepped into his house to get his bags. He loved her sweet, surprised laughter when she looked at all his suitcases, journals, newspaper clippings, old books, music sheets, and vinyl records. Their long kisses and soft yet strong lovemaking on his bed. The depth of a tranquil night, by her side. Their first shared meal at his house. Him wanting her to stay longer, to love her again and again, and Marlui pressing him to move on, to leave the city and take the road, so that she could return to her beloved woods.

After crossing a bridge over a large river, Marlui told Thomas to drive through a dirt road. On the left side, he could see patches of corn plantations, on the right, the thick forest green.

"Stop the car, Thomas!" Marlui said, startling him.

By the side of the road, three kids struggled to carry a huge bundle.

"These are my cousins," she said. "Let's give them a ride."

Thomas was impressed by the flexible, fast moves of the kids as they got into the car, pulling their large bundle along with them. They were laughing, and Marlui joined in with them and cracked up after they told her something in their native tongue.

Curious, Thomas parked the car so he could look in the back seat. He wasn't expecting to see the armadillo's tiny, dark head. "What? Is he alive?"

"Of course, he is," Marlui said. "They are not hunting it; all they want is for the armadillo to move his home away."

Thomas felt as if he had crossed some invisible gateway into somewhere new, a place where things happened according to laws he couldn't really grasp.

"Yes," said one of the kids. "We want to play soccer by the forest, and this armadillo just loves to make his holes in the field we have chosen for the game. He will enjoy his new home. It is very close by, just a bit farther from us."

"He won't mind the change. We know it," said the girl.

"I am not so sure about that," Marlui told the kids. "If he comes back to his regular spot, you must leave him alone, okay? And you must play around his holes."

Thomas started driving again, laughing to himself as he realized he had fallen deeply in love with a girl who cared so much for an armadillo's wishes.

HOME

Thomas parked the car on a clearing under the trees. Marlui greeted a very old man who was carrying some wood on his back. His muscles were shining under the sun, and his moves were steady, albeit a bit slow.

"Marlui, shouldn't we help him?" asked Thomas.

"Of course not," she told him. "He would be offended. This is his job."

"How old is he?" asked Thomas.

"I don't really know. Maybe eighty."

Marlui took Thomas by the hand and helped him carry his luggage. His guitar hung on his back as he followed her. He found his gaze settling on the colorful tattoos that covered the young people's bodies, rushing forward to greet them. They were beautiful. They spontaneously introduced themselves and addressed Marlui in their native tongue first before they turned to Thomas.

"We like your music. We have seen you on the internet. Sometimes we play your videos. They are very good."

They left Thomas's luggage in Marlui's house, a little hut beautifully adorned with colorful pieces of cloth spread all over the walls, covering the windows. On a tiny straw table, he saw her laptop and journals. Piles of books were spread over a couple of handcrafted, wooden nightstands. Her large, high, wooden double bed seemed to occupy most of the space, and some carpets had been spread over the dirt floor.

Lovely sculptures of animals were sitting by her laptop. Thomas took the tiny armadillo in his hands and smiled.

"This is my mother's work. They are so cute, aren't they?" said Marlui.

He saw a couple of long, beautifully carved pipes next to the tiny statues. "Do you smoke these pipes, Marlui? Are they yours?"

"Yes, I carved those pipes myself. But I can't say I smoke them like people do in the cities. These are sacred instruments. They are used to smoke consecrated herbs and to call upon our spiritual guides."

Thomas threw himself on Marlui's bed. It felt so soft and fluffy. He inhaled the soft scent of herbs and flowers.

"Oh, dear, we have company," she said, pulling her gaze away from him.

A tall, slim dog jumped on top of the bed and sat by Thomas. He was startled at first, but when the dog licked his face, he laughed.

"This is Jagua, my dearest friend and faithful companion," Marlui said.

Jagua moved on to their feet, and Thomas embraced Marlui tenderly. They kept quiet and motionless over the bed for a few seconds. At a loss for words, Thomas realized Marlui did not actually expect him to court her in a conventional way. He felt as if she could sense his feelings just by touch. She kissed him on the mouth, and afterward, she cupped his face and stared into his eyes.

Tears sprung from Thomas's eyes and trailed down his face. "What has happened to me, Marlui? Why has my music left me? I could see the dancing creatures around the kids. I can glimpse them hovering over you now, but they won't come near me anymore. I miss them so much. You see, when I lost my parents, the pain was unbearable. I was no longer a child like all the others.

I felt cut off from life. I did not want to play, to study, to have a regular childhood. All I cherished was the company of my secret creatures of sound. They have kept me alive."

Marlui sat on her bed and breathed a deep sigh. She was quiet for a few moments, slowly kissing Thomas's head. When she opened her mouth, ready to speak, the curtain at the entrance was opened, and someone's head popped in. He had strong deep eyes, straight, thick hair, and a smoking pipe in his mouth.

"May I help him a little?" the young man asked.

"Yes, of course. This is my brother, Wera," she said to Thomas. "Come on in!"

Thomas rose from the bed, and Jagua, the dog, left the hut while Marlui and her brother spoke to each other.

Then she translated Wera's words so Thomas would understand. "Our father is coming to see you, Thomas. But my brother thinks we should cleanse you first. Can we do that?"

"Cleanse? I took a shower this morning, remember? I didn't feel dirty . . . but, oh . . . yes, just do what you have to do."

Marlui took a small stool and sat right in front of her brother and Thomas.

Wera looked at Thomas and cleared his throat. "Please, sit on the bed and close your eyes."

Thomas did as he was told. He could smell the sweet aroma of herbs when Wera blew smoke over the top of his head. He could hear a musical prayer whispered around his ears. He could feel Wera's hands pressing over the top of his head, and he enjoyed their warmth. Suddenly, he could see himself as a child again. There he was, opening the door to his house for the first time after his parents passed. He experienced the same fear, pain, emptiness, and perplexity he had back then. The word "home" had lost its meaning. He found himself in an empty house. A hollow feeling turned into shivers, and he froze as he crossed the hall to his bedroom. Thomas tried to shake away the painful memories, but Wera's strong hands over his head stopped him from moving away. Then he saw them again. The secret creatures of sound. And not only them, but he could also see himself as a little lost boy, getting in touch with these musical beings for the very first time. Past and present mingled, and a new dimension of time presented itself in his mind and heart. He involuntarily opened up his eyes. There she was, Marlui. Eyes and mouth wide open, staring at the air above his head. He knew she had shared his vision. She had seen his past, his present, and now all he wanted was for her to share his future.

He felt a sudden urge to thank Wera so much for reconnecting him to his musical companions. He stood up to hug him.

"Please, don't you touch me now . . ." Wera told him, quickly moving out of the way.

Thomas was hurt, startled, feeling lost again. He turned to Marlui to ask for an explanation, but Wera quickly added:

"My spirit is very tired. I have given you all I could. I need to rest for a while. So sorry. We can talk later."

Then somebody else stepped into her hut—a man with white, long hair, piercing eyes, and dark brown skin. The man stood there in silence, taking him in from head to toe. He also smoked a long pipe. His strong figure stood motionless.

"I know you. You were the one in the woods," Thomas said.

Marlui stepped forward and smiled at the man. "Thomas, this is my grandpa, Popygua."

THE INVITE

Thomas and Marlui stepped out of the house to greet the elderly man.

Popygua nodded at him. "Nice to meet you in the flesh, young man."

Thomas looked down at the grass, not knowing if he should ask about this so-called previous meeting. Finally, he made up his mind. "I don't understand, sir. I remember seeing you near the trees, outside Dr. Alonso's house. But it did not seem real. I mean, I had a vision, or maybe a daydream. How could that be?"

"Yes, I did travel to see you. I mean, spiritually. You may not believe my words, all these ancient forms of communication such as speaking without words, dream making, spiritual journeys—they're discredited by your people, the 'civilized' ones. Yet, they remain alive among us."

Marlui smiled at her grandpa. The three of them stood face-to-face for a few seconds, then Popygua said, "Thomas, come with me. Let's take a walk."

Thomas turned to invite Marlui to come along, but she had already gone back to her house.

"Jagua is hungry. I need to feed him now," she called from the doorway.

Thomas realized he had to follow Popygua. To his surprise, the old man walked very swiftly, leading him into the forest. Thomas tripped over rocks, stumbled over the roots, and awkwardly tried to keep up with Popygua's smooth steps. Feeling like a clumsy little toddler, Thomas laughed at himself.

"Good. You are laughing again. This is good," mumbled Popygua ahead of him.

Lush, green leaves seemed to caress Thomas's skin as he crossed the narrow path, lizards slid next to his feet, and birds and monkeys moved over his head in the treetops. Thomas hopped over a stream, finally feeling more at ease, his whole body refreshed by the fresh air and the sudden awareness of walking amidst so many lively beings. A few steps ahead, standing by the riverbank, Popygua waited for him.

As Thomas approached, Popygua sat on a patch of grass and gestured for him to do the same.

"Just close your eyes, my boy. You need some sun on you."

At first, Thomas was uncomfortable sitting by the old man, not knowing what to say or how to act. He let the sunrays spread over his face and arms like a pleasant, healing balm. He inhaled the delicious aroma of fresh sparkling water and slowly felt the astute, subtle motion of the soft shifting waves as they mesmerized him.

There, the young musician and the ancient healer sat for a long time. Thomas felt so peaceful. He remained motionless, not wanting to break the harmony of such a soothing experience.

Finally, Popygua spoke, "According to our beliefs, people have a double body. It is not the same as a spirit, or a soul, in the way you people from the outside call it. For us, each living being has a double."

Thomas stared at Popygua's face, unable to see his eyes, as the old man continued to stare at the river.

"How many riverbanks can you see, Thomas?"

"I can see our bank, here, where we are sitting, and the other side, at a distance," said Thomas.

"Well, a river also has a double, as do the trees, the animals, and, of course, you and me. When you were in danger, I sent my double to shield you. Now, the people you were with did not mean to harm you physically. They knew better than that. What they wanted was to capture your double. Your spirit, if you prefer to call it that."

Thomas was at a loss for words, as he had been so many times since meeting Marlui.

Popygua went on. "You still need healing, you know. Your heart has hidden so much pain over the years. That is why those people got ahold of you. On the outside, you look young and powerful, but there is a breach in you. If you don't become one with yourself, someone else will find the space to break you again."

Thomas moved so he was face-to-face with Popygua. "Popygua, do you mean they will try to steal my music?"

Popygua rose to his feet and laughed heartily. "Your music? Does the sun belong to you? Do the stars belong to you?"

Night was falling, and the first stars twinkled across the light-blue sky. Popygua went back to the forest. Thomas hurried his steps, trying to keep up with him again, listening intently.

"Dear boy, we belong to the Earth. Not the other way around. Trees are alive, they speak, they sing, and they chose you to hear them when you were a little boy. You did not come here by chance."

"Please, sir, tell me more about that. This is all so new to me," said Thomas.

Popygua would not answer any more questions. He walked in silence, Thomas following, back to Marlui's house. She greeted them with a large smile.

Popygua stood by her door, and he said, "Young man, you are invited to come and sing at the prayer house. I will wait for you there tonight, around eight."

"It will be an honor, Popygua!"

Thomas felt as if a heavy burden had been lifted from his shoulders. He smiled, feeling so young, like a small boy with so much to learn. Marlui had fixed a meal while he'd been by the riverbank. He sat at her small table and enjoyed every single bite.

TOP SHELVES

Vera walked into her flat, took a shower, had a snack, and went into her mother's office. Her four-bedroom flat had been decorated according to her strict, elegant rules—light beige walls, a few comfy couches, glass tables, and a high-tech kitchen. Yet, she had kept her mother's favorite place as she had loved it. The shining mahogany desk, the old blue globe, her crescent moon divan sitting against the mauve walls. Most of all, she had kept her mother's shelves exactly as they had been, with all the bric-a-brac—the Russian dolls, her collection of pendulums, her beautiful, translucent crystals, and her delicate statutes.

As a child, Vera had fallen in love with the kaleidoscopes, the collection of tarot cards, and her mother's exquisite mirrors over the desk. *I wish I could introduce Mom to my new friends. Their kids would love her*, she thought.

Vera raised her eyes toward the top shelves. She knew they held her mother's powerful magic books. Her mother even had her own private magical name, Maya. It meant *the illusion*. Sitting at the desk, Vera touched the crystals, and it suddenly dawned on her how unusual her parents' relationship would seem today. She had never seen a couple like them. Her father was a down-to-earth lawyer and her mother a mystical, dreamy, sensitive woman. Maybe their personalities were complementary; even so, they seemed to love each other so very much. As their only daughter, Vera felt much closer to her father's beliefs and his attitude toward life than her mother's.

My parents would never have met these days, she thought. *No app would be able to put them together, as they were two separate, distinct personalities.* "Like-minded people?" Vera looked at her own reflection in the mirror. *That sounds like fascism to me. Vive la différence*, she thought.

Vera lifted her mobile from the desk and texted Jonas.

> *We must talk about Dr. Alonso.*
> *You are right. He has to be stopped.*
> *What shall we do about it?*

THE MUSIC OF THE TREES

Sitting on a small, carved stool just outside Marlui's house, Thomas played with the strings of his guitar. A sweet, unfamiliar melody seemed to echo through the trees, reaching out to his fingers to play it. As he followed his musical impulse, his feet started to tap on the dirt, and he began mumbling sounds. Next to Thomas, crouched over a spot of grass, Marlui carved a tiny little leopard. When her eyes left the statuette for a few seconds, Thomas noticed her retinas enlarge as she silently stared at the sunset. Maybe, in another moment, in a different scenario, he would start chatting; there were so many things Thomas wanted to share with her. Yet, he was afraid his voice would somehow disrupt the harmony of their silent exchange. He concentrated on translating the intriguing forest sounds through music.

Marlui was the one who spoke first. "So, you can hear the music of the trees now?"

Thomas kept on playing delicately, whispering, "In a way . . . yes."

"Grandpa says, at the beginning of life, all beings could hear each other's music. There was hardly any need for chatting or debating; people just sang, blending their voices with the sounds of the forest and all living beings. People would suffer and cry at the screams of a dying tree during its fall, rejoice and sing along with the bird's tunes, and, most of all, speak the language of the wind. Why did they refuse to listen to nature later on?

"We see all original forest nations as our relatives. Each nation has its own myths and traditions, yet some things remain sacred among us, such as reverence for forests. Anyway, the other day, I heard a relative of ours tell Grandpa that some people were not from the Earth, originally, but from a distant star. This is why they felt no connection to the trees, mountains, rivers, or animals. This is also why they felt superior, entitled to rule over all types of life, not to mention, to destroy them for their own purposes. What is comfort, anyway? Having it all brand new? As a relative of ours likes to say, 'People can't actually eat gold.'"

Thomas stopped playing and interrupted Marlui. "The stars. Look at them. So beautiful to look at on a clear dusk. I love to see the stars and the moon shifting places with the sun at twilight. Anyway, Dr. Alonso and his Orphics believe they should revere a specific constellation—Orpheus's. There must be some lost link between these myths, I mean, between your narratives and the ancient Greek ones."

Marlui stood up, stared at Thomas with smiling eyes, and said, "Ancient, we are, indeed. Very ancient, in fact. Some people call us underdeveloped. I say lots of humans nowadays are actually degenerating, not evolving, as they claim."

Thomas left the stool and followed Marlui into her house. "How so?" He asked.

"Is pollution a sign of evolution? Segregation? Violence among the young ones? Racism? To me, it all sounds like decay. We respect your science, we use some of your technology, but I wish you would do the same with our traditional knowledge."

Thomas waited for Marlui to put on a beautiful cotton dress, then he spoke again. "The other day, I heard an Eastern sage say that if people could see the overall mosaic of life's knowledge, they would realize everything could be complementary. I know this is utopian, but I like to keep it in mind anyway."

Marlui kissed Thomas and hugged him tight. "It's my dream, too. But for now, let's sing at the praying house. It is beautiful. I am sure you'll enjoy it."

"Should I take my guitar along?" asked Thomas.

"Do you want to?" asked Marlui, kissing him again.

"I feel as if I am beginning to grasp new songs and melodies. I would love to play them."

Marlui put on her sandals and crossed the small path through the trees. People were leaving their houses to join the prayers, and Thomas followed them. After a few steps, he could already hear some strong, vibrant singing.

MYSTERIOUS DREAMS

Gabriella loved dusting bookshelves at dusk. She knew it did not seem to be a conventional habit, in the sense that most of her friends would rather clean the house early in the morning. Not her. She loved getting up, fixing breakfast, and writing. Dreams always brought her ideas, scenes, dialogues, an unusual atmosphere that called for words. On the other hand, she believed the kids' room should be properly organized for them to fall asleep and have their own dreams. So, in her very personal routine, dusk was the best time for cleaning. After that, she loved fixing dinner, which she usually did with Jonas's help. She considered him a much better cook than herself.

She collected the boys' new drawings. André could already write a few words and sentences, so his drawings carried some strange names, and she smiled when she took a few moments to appreciate them. Now, Manuel was more interested in painting vibrant colors. Together, the boys enjoyed inventing all sorts of strange creatures. There was a method to it. Manuel chose parts of old, broken toys to put together. As the new creature was made, André immediately drew it so they could name it together. Their new invention was a crazy, lovely little singing dragon. He had a fierce, spitting-fire mouth, yet his huge eyes were just sheer love.

Gabriella took the new artwork from their small table and pinned them on the cupboard. Next, she collected their favorite books, spread all over their beds, and put them neatly on the bedside tables. She could easily distinguish the different tastes and personalities. André loved fairy tales, and Manuel loved animals, including their habits and habitats.

Sometimes, Gabriella loved being surprised by her kids' mysterious dreams, inventions, and unexpected decisions, just like when they insisted they would meet a friend at the square. Listening to them had led her to meet so many new friends. How could that be? Why do children sometimes seem to tap into a wisdom that adults apparently lose on their way through life?

Her cell rang; she answered Vera's call.

"Good news, my dear! Jonas and I have already spoken to both his students' families, and they've agreed to make a complaint against Dr. Alonso for psychological abuse and charlatanism. We should ask Thomas for his consent so that he can be included as well."

Gabriella sat on her children's bed, and for a few seconds, she was overwhelmed by the strong desire to protect her kids from all types of abuse throughout their lives. "Marlui has taken Thomas to her community, in the reserved area of the forest. But she usually answers her email so . . ."

"Why don't we go there tomorrow morning? I am sure your boys would love to meet Marlui and Thomas again. She has invited us over, remember?" suggested Vera.

"Yes, that is a great idea."

"I do think we must hurry. Dr. Alonso has been known for his long leave of absences. All he has to do is take a sabbatical for a year and go to some other country. I was told he has mansions in several other countries."

"Is that so? He really sounds like a millionaire action-movie villain. Life imitates art, or should it be the other way around?" said Gabriella with a smirk.

"Villain or charlatan, whatever," said Vera. "Your husband is very optimistic about defeating Dr. Alonso. I am not. However, there will be small talk at the university. His prestige will be tainted, and for me, as long as he keeps away from young, talented people, I will be happy."

FIVE STRINGS

"His voice is as strong and beautiful as I dreamt it would be." Thomas sat on a wooden bench next to Marlui and several other young people from her community. Thick, smoky shadows circulated around the bodies of several other singers slowly moving inside the empty space of the praying house. He had expected to be taken to a regular temple, full of statues and sculptures, maybe intricate mosaic drawings on the floor. But no. Clay walls and a straw roof covered a totally empty space. At its center, there was a stool on which a lovely girl sat with her eyes closed while Popygua puffed clouds of smoke over her head.

"Listen," said Marlui. "This is a healing ceremony."

Thomas watched while a few young people slowly danced around Popygua, smoking their pipes, eyes closed, movements so precise they would not stumble or fall.

"Can I join them?" asked Thomas.

"No. Unless Grandpa invites you to do it. You should not touch them either. Their senses are heightened now," said Marlui.

Some kids sat on a straw mat and started playing drums. Three others played guitars. The music was mesmerizing, somehow echoing the melodious fragments Thomas had been playing that afternoon. The slow, invigorating rhythm seemed to bring waves of enthusiasm and instant happiness to his heart.

"This is so amazing," he kept on saying, over and over, no matter how many times Marlui begged him to keep quiet.

Popygua gestured to the girl to leave her seat and rest on an empty straw mat. He smiled at Thomas and approached him. "Welcome, my boy."

Thomas held his guitar, touched its strings, and would not stop talking. He told Popygua, "This is so fantastic! The singing, the magical atmosphere. I feel renewed already. I have been healed. I feel so good. I want to be a part of this ceremony. Can I play while you sing, Popygua? I would really be honored. I want to be able to share this moment with all of you. It would be my sincere gift, my contribution."

Popygua interrupted Thomas, "No. You cannot play."

"No?" Thomas felt a myriad of emotions—disappointment, despair, deep rejection, and yet, there was also a weird, unexpected sense of relief.

"Just listen, my boy. You must listen again . . . that's all."

At a loss for words, Thomas placed his six-string guitar over his lap and listened. Popygua went back to the center of the circle and sang with full lungs. His voice was no longer human, resonating the cry of some mythical and eternal bird.

Thomas's whole body shivered, and he closed his eyes. There he was—flying over the treetops. He could hear every single movement of the monkeys jumping over the benches. He could hear a million birds' songs. He could capture the subtle music emanating from the dew falling over shining leaves. The snapping trunks seemed to send him reassuring messages of peace. His eyes captured new shades of color in the night, grass spread out in front of him, and he felt his body running so fast, crossing tracks, sniffing scents and floral aromas. He opened his eyes again, expecting to find himself back in the praying house with Marlui, but what greeted him were his two naked feet on a dirt floor. His toes started to grow, to reach into the earth and spread themselves as long roots. What should feel like a nightmare was just the opposite. For the first time in his entire life, Thomas felt such a piercing will to really live and experience life and its true meaning. All he wanted to do was sit there and *be* . . .

All of a sudden, Thomas heard a distinct twang as one of his guitar strings broke by itself, as if it had a life of its own.

Thomas opened his eyes. Popygua sat in front of him, laughing.

"We only play with five strings, you know. This is how we were taught at the beginning of time. The voice of the forest only needs five strings. Now your guitar is ready to speak to us. Play it, please. Play for us."

Thomas stood up, walked toward the drummers and other guitar players on the mat, and started to play. For the first time, he realized that his secret creatures of sound had always dwelled inside his heart, and it was his openness that welcomed them to him.

At that moment, he felt one with the forest, with all creatures, with the river, with the stars, and with all that is.

THOMAS'S JOURNAL

SIX NEW ABILITIES

Now I can see with my eyes closed.

Now I can hear with my fingertips.

Now I can smell without breathing.

Now I can taste flavors without eating food.

Now I can feel things without touching them.

Now I can sense all senses, even when they don't make any sense.

SO SIMPLE AND TRUE

"Can I jump in?" Thomas asked.

Marlui addressed the kids in her native tongue and turned to Thomas. "Yes, they want to swim with you. Go on, Thomas."

The river waters were shimmering green. The six kids were already in there, splashing water all around and laughing at their jumping dogs. The midday sun was burning Thomas's shoulders, and he dove deeply. There were no currents; the waters flowed softly. He tried his best crawl movements and crossed to the other side very quickly. He came out on the riverbank and realized none of the kids had followed him.

"C'mon. Let's compete! I will give a prize to the best swimmer."

The kids didn't jump into the river, just the opposite. They left the water and sat on the sand and started speaking amongst themselves. Thomas called Marlui. "Why won't they come?"

The young woman dove and crossed the river under the waters. She reminded Thomas of a mythical siren as she moved through the water, although there was nothing dangerous about her. Then she tossed her long, wet hair back over her shoulders, before sitting next to Thomas. "Kids here don't like competing," she said.

"How so? Every child likes to be the first," said Thomas.

Marlui laughed and kissed his wet cheeks."Not us. Kids are taught to always wait for the slower ones. Especially when swimming in the river waters."

Thomas kept quiet for a few seconds. "Sorry. You are right. It makes so much sense. By the way, everything here sounds so simple and true to me. Can I stay with you? At least for a while?" he asked.

She held him for a few minutes before pulling back and looking into his eyes. "Won't you mind living by our way? I mean, you will not have the same comforts you have been used to. No en suite bathrooms, no fine cuisine, no pampering whatsoever . . ."

Thomas kissed Marlui's mouth, interrupting her before he answered, "I will be very comfortable. Emotionally comfortable, I mean. I have been feeling so peaceful, so creative, so grounded since arriving here."

Marlui looked at the river and felt herself overflowing with joy. She smiled and waved at the kids on the opposite bank. They were already leaving for lunch.

"I have been thinking about Orpheus," said Thomas, "winning over the beasts in hell with the beauty of his music. Now I can see the obvious: the myth speaks about one's inner wastelands. Popygua has taught me the healing songs. It is not about empowerment, but being able to share, to receive, to accept the gifts of life. What I mean is that maybe I could also use some of my expertise and resources to share the beauty of your tradition."

Marlui held Thomas by his shoulders, kissed him, and said, "I must tell you something. I don't really like this Eurydice character very much."

"How so?" asked Thomas.

Marlui laughed. "She is so weak, so submissive. Why didn't she just flee from hell and meet Orpheus outside? I would have. There's something else too. Hades did not forbid her to speak to Orpheus, as far as I know. So, all she had to do was say something, to give her lover a reassuring signal so he had no reason to turn around. She could even have touched him or thrown a stone on the path. None of us girls here would have been so stupid. But, of course, it is just a story."

AS ABOVE, SO BELOW

"I knew it! I just knew it!!"

Jonas complained in the van all the way to the forest. Vera drove silently, and the kids played in the back seat while Gabriella listened to him.

"Dr. Alonso has already fled. He is out in the world, somewhere. At least I heard rumors about his resignation. The atmosphere in college will be much better without having him around, that's for sure."

Gabriella handed her boys two bottles of water and turned to Jonas. "Don't you feel he should be punished, somehow?"

Vera huffed. "He is very powerful, and he will find ways to try to evade, postpone, and deny the accusations of misconduct and so on. But at least his reputation has been tainted and young students will not be recruited as easily as they used to be. Besides, Dr. Alonso is very vain, and I am sure he is not happy about all the posts and photos denouncing him on social media. He will have to live a secluded life. No more prestigious parties, no more lectures, international invitations."

"So, at least there's a good reason to celebrate."

"Yes," said Jonas. "Most of all, Thomas seems to be fine. Don't you think this is such good news?"

Vera smiled and looked at the forest trees by the road. "'*The world is full of magic things, patiently waiting for our senses to grow sharper*,' says W.B. Yeats, one of my mother's favorite poets."

"Stop the car." Both boys shouted at the same time, and Vera stomped on the brakes. "Look! There are kids in the forest."

As Vera pulled over on the dirt road, André and Manuel opened the door and jumped out of the car.

Gabriella noticed three kids, two boys and a girl, jumping down from the branches of a tree. Their smiling faces were so lovely. She greeted them. "Hello."

"Are you heading to Marlui's house?" the girl asked. "We can take you there."

"Yes, we want to ride in your car. It is so big!" said the boy.

Vera opened the back door, and all five kids climbed inside. The girl gave directions while the two other kids exchanged some words in their native language. André and Manuel just laughed, happy.

All of a sudden, they heard it, the music. They could identify Thomas's melodies immediately, although it sounded stronger, somewhat more harmoniously raw.

Gabriella took mental notes as she saw Thomas playing his guitar, surrounded by two other musicians, both of them very young. Standing in front of him, an elderly man sang lyrics she could not understand, although she immediately guessed they were prayers.

Her boys followed their new friends and sat around the musicians by the campfire. They were clapping hands and humming to the melody as if they had known it for a long time.

She thought about ancient Greece and the tragic myths she had loved so much as a little girl. She remembered the gods, the demigods, their crazy power plays always reverberating over human life. Orpheus and the power of music, an overwhelming myth, still underlying the lives of so many talented souls.

Listening to that unique sound that morning, the word *power* seemed to lose its meaning. Gabriella decided that, from that moment on, the verbs *owning* and *having* would have to be replaced with *being*. She wanted to listen to the forest legends. And in her next narratives, there would be no dualities but the merging of antagonistic views. Maybe plots would have to be rediscovered, reinvented as a way of stories. In the clearing, by the fire, surrounded by music, sitting next to her loved ones, she realized the word *family* meant all types of beings, being at the center of life's *Emerald Table*. As above, so below . . .

Afterword

When we observe the indigenous life and how it is still lived,
what most people think is poverty—for indigenous people—is
actually an achievement. It's wholeness, the integrity of being,
the wholeness of being. They are whole beings because they are
beings who walk on this earth upon which we tread and take
our physical energy whilst communicating with the universe, the
cosmos. Indigenous people maintain this equilibrium. This gives
me really good hope.
–Daniel Munduruku,
award-winning Brazilian writer and educator.

Edgy, restless as a typical hyperactive boy, my father, Luiz Prieto, relaxed and had a great time while playing with kids at the Guarani village near my grandparents, on the shore of São Vicente, Brazil, back in 1940.

All through his life, he looked upon indigenous traditions as a source of wisdom and peace. "When the world is ravished due to human foolishness, indigenous people will be the new leaders because only they can follow the path of the stars," he used to tell me. His search for inner balance led him to yearly travels to the Xavante's community. On his part, he tried to meet with some of their demands, such as bringing them musical equipment to record their sacred songs. My granny Leonor believed my father healed and restored himself at every stay and exchange.

I inherited his deep admiration for the forest dwellers in Brazil. As an adult, when I became a professional writer, I had the opportunity to work with award-winning writer Daniel Munduruku in his brilliant book, *Tales of the Forest*. It was the beginning of a long-lasting friendship and creative partnership. For thirty years now, I have been translating indigenous tales, curating books about their traditions of wisdom, giving creative writing workshops, traveling with them, and most of all, learning from these enlightened friends of mine.

Writing *The Musician* was my way of paying homage to their traditions and trying to convey some of my own experience through the characters and plot.

As in my father's case, my perception of the world has been deeply influenced by the teachings of Guarani *Chamois*—contemplation of nature, the eloquence of silence and the ability to laugh at myself while learning from my mistakes. Last year, Karai Papa Mirim, the healer whom my mother also used to visit, called me his relative. This is the greatest compliment I could ever have received.

A few years back, Estas Tonne, an extraordinarily gifted musician and a dear long-time friend now, came to Brazil. He played his magical guitar at the Guarani praying house. It was such a memorable moment that I tried to convey some of its enchantment in a chapter entitled "Five Strings." During the musician's creative process, Estas and I exchanged ideas and perceptions about the healing gift of music, and this is how the story unfolded in my imagination.

I hope this tale has resonated within you and that it remains in your memory so that you may "see" all that there is, even with your eyes closed.

Acknowledgments

I would like to thank Greg Fields for his kindness and enthusiastic support, Harry Browne, the Inkies, Ciaran O'Melia, Angelina Kelly, Davey Inthevalley, and dearest Claire Galligan.

Special thanks to John Koehler for having believed in this magical tale.

Thanks to Victor Scatolin for his literary exchange, edits, translation (Portuguese/French/English) and, most of all, for the "transcreation" of Gérard de Nerval's poem, "El Desdichado," attributed to Thomas, *The Musician*.

To Estas Tonne, I want to express my gratitude for his readings, suggestions, creative support, and his inspiring music, this novel's secret soundtrack.

Lightning Source UK Ltd.
Milton Keynes UK
UKHW010719131222
413853UK00001B/23